The Day the Fire Came

Dorcas Wilson

Visit us online at www.authorsonline.co.uk

A Bright Pen Book

British Library Cataloguing in Publication Data.
A catalogue record for this book is available from the British Library.

ISBN 978-0-7552-1644-4

Authors OnLine Ltd
19 The Cinques
Gamlingay, Sandy
Bedfordshire SG19 3NU
England

This book is also available in e-book format, details of which are available at www.authorsonline.co.uk

Chapter 1

Mary was in the woods, although she knew she would get into trouble for being there – especially as she was meant to be fetching water from the well – but she didn't care. She loved being in the woods, even when like today it was threatening to rain; in fact, she particularly liked the woods when rain threatened: the dark, the calm before the rain began, gave the woods a peaceful almost magical feeling. She would spend hours out here, amongst the trees, listening to the birds singing, the trickling of the stream, the sound of the animals in the undergrowth.

For some weeks now she had not been out in the woods as her parents said it was too dangerous with all the soldiers about. So what? There had been soldiers about for as long as she could remember. They would ride through the village on their way to and from England; sometimes they were English, sometimes Scottish. She didn't care what the fighting was about. Her father had tried to explain to her how Robert Bruce had taken the Scottish throne but King Edward of England wanted the throne himself. But she hadn't shown any interest; she didn't care who was king. What she cared about was that after a village near them had been attacked by soldiers her parents had banned her from playing in the woods.

'It's not safe. What would you do if the soldiers came and you were out there all alone?' her mother would say when she pleaded to be allowed to go to the woods.

The soldiers come! The soldiers wouldn't come. Why would they? The other village had been attacked because they had refused to provide food for the soldiers. Their village always gave when asked. 'Our village would be left alone,' she had said defiantly. Her mother had turned away, quiet and worried looking. Mary didn't understand why her mother would be worried, until out here in the woods it came to her.

A few weeks back she had been wakened by the sounds of people talking loudly and had opened her eyes in time to see her father and brother leaving with two armed men.

'Father!' she had shouted, jumping out of bed.

Alarmed by her shout, the two men had turned and stared at her, one with a concerned look on his face, the other with a malevolent look that he quickly replaced with a false smile.

'Back to bed, Mary,' her mother had ordered, helping her back into bed and pulling the blanket up round her shoulders. 'Go to sleep and don't worry.'

She had lain awake; where had her father and brother gone? Who were the armed men? Were they soldiers taking them to be executed? But then her mother hadn't seemed too concerned. Surely if her husband and son were being arrested her mother would have been upset? No, that couldn't have been it. But where were they being taken? Would she see them again? If not, it would be up to her to help her mother tend to the land and look after the animals. It would be hard work, but she would do it. She would need to learn to chop firewood and to kill the wild animals that attacked their cattle. She would need to get a knife, a proper one, not the small one she had been given last year, but one like Malcolm's. Just as she had determined to work hard and help her mother the best she could, her father and brother returned.

'Where did you go last night?' she had asked, Malcolm the next morning.

‘One of the neighbours was ill and needed help,’ he replied quickly. She had spent that day looking carefully at their neighbours; none of them looked ill.

The following night, she had lain awake to see if her father and brother would go out again. As darkness fell, Malcolm and her father rose quietly, and taking food and ale with them, sneaked out into the night. They returned sometime later, cold, wet and shivering. She had thought it strange that they were wet when it hadn’t rained for days. She couldn’t figure it out and any time she asked, the subject was quickly changed.

She didn’t care. Out here, in the woods, she could be free. This is where she came when she was angry, happy or sad. Where she came to dream of all the places she had heard about from the beggars who passed through the village as they wandered from town to town. She loved to hear their descriptions of the sights, sounds and smell of the towns. She wanted to experience them all herself. She wanted adventure and excitement.

It was different for Malcolm. He would become a farmer and a soldier, fight all over the country or even go on a crusade. The most she could hope for was marriage to another peasant and maybe a monthly trip to town for market day. Would she ever get to see the sights and sounds of the big towns, would she ever smell the smells, even the disgusting ones like the smell of dead bodies left to rot, the smell of…? She sniffed the air. She sniffed, again. The smell of smoke followed by distant screams coming from the direction of the village brought her out of her dream. Quickly, all thought of the towns gone, dread growing with every step, she ran home. Despite her growing fears, she tried to convince herself that the smoke came from a fire, set by one of the villagers that had got out of control and the screams the results of innocent fun. On reaching the edge of the woods, the sound of roaring flames, the smoke swirling amongst the trees and the sight of her village burning showed that her mother had been right; the soldiers had come.

'Mother, father, Malcolm!' she screamed, heading into the smoke, stopping only when her eyes stung and tears streamed down her face. All around her were shapeless, shifting shadows. A large shadow bore down on her. Frozen to the spot she stared, unsure what was speeding towards her. A demon? A man? She lifted her feet but they were like lead. No matter how hard she tried, she could not get out of the way. The shadow was getting closer, silent except for a strange thudding sound. It was almost on her. With one last effort, her feet came away from the ground and she flung herself to the side as the demon flew past her.

Frightened, she ran back into the woods. Left and right, twisting and turning; she went round in circles. Not knowing what direction she was heading in, tripping over the tree roots that stretched across the path, she kept on going. She turned one way, then another, moving deeper into the forest with every turn and growing more afraid with every step. Until, soaking wet, covered in mud, hair dripping, her clothes sticking to her, she stumbled across the moss covered trunk of a long fallen tree. Staggering, tripping over a rabbit that darted out in front of her, she threw herself onto the trunk. Too exhausted to care that it was still raining, too exhausted to move.

As she sat, the sky darkened and the trees seemed to close in on her. She thought she could see demons lurking in the shadows. The singing of the birds sounded like the screams of her family and neighbours, the sound of animals moving in the undergrowth became soldiers creeping up on her. The sound of the wind blowing through the trees reminded her of the flames. Too afraid to run or move, she stared into the night until she fell asleep.

'Don't be afraid.' The sound of a woman's voice, gentle and soft, followed by the touch of a hand on her shoulder wakened her.

'Thank you,' Mary murmured, still half asleep, as she sunk further into the cloak that had been placed round her shoulders.

'Hae a drink.' A man standing in front of her handed her a leather flask. Slowly, she raised the flask to her lips and drank. As soon as she had swallowed the unpleasant tasting liquor, her throat burned and her eyes watered.

'Hae anither drink, it'll stop you shiverin'.' Reluctantly she obeyed; this time the drink went down easier.

Her eyes having adjusted to the morning sun, and feeling revived by the warmth of the cloak and the ale, she was able to take in the people around her. There wasn't one man but two rough, long haired men standing in front; they were identical. They were short and stocky with reddish brown hair, their beards matted and tangled. Their shirts slashed and cut, one had been ripped from the shoulder, a blood soaked bandage protruding through the tear. Swords and daggers hung from their belts. Confused, her head spinning from the liquor and the cold, she tried to figure out who they were and why they were helping her. Maybe they were soldiers returning from attacking her village, lulling her into a false sense of comfort before striking. She looked again at the men. They looked tough. They had big shiny, sharp weapons - if they were going to attack her she wouldn't have a chance against them, but they had friendly eyes; she would trust them. She had no other choice.

'Who are you?' she asked weakly.

'I'm Duncan,' the man who had handed her the drink introduced himself. 'He's Donald.' He pointed at his companion, who nodded.

'An' she's Belle.' Donald indicated the woman who was crouching by her side. Mary glanced at her. The woman had long hair pulled back carelessly, leaving a few locks falling over her kindly face; she wore a shirt that appeared to be a couple of sizes too big.

'What are you doing out here alone?' Belle spoke softly.

'I don't know,' she cried, the tears mixing with the rain water running down her face.

'Where have you come from?' Belle asked soothingly.

'My village. Burnt to the ground.'

'How'd you manage to get awa'?' Donald or maybe it was Duncan, she didn't know which, asked.

Mary stared at him for a few seconds before she spoke. When she found her voice, the words came all at once, 'I wasn't there, I was in the woods, I was dreaming of adventures. I smelt smoke. I saw a demon. I ran, I ran.' Stopping for breath, she laid her head in her hands and cried.

'Wait here, we'll not hurt you,' Belle whispered before moving off to one side with Duncan and Donald. Mary could hear them whispering but couldn't make out what they were saying.

Belle returned to her side. 'You can't stay out here alone. You must come with us.' The twins nodded their agreement.

'Who are you?' was all she could say.

'Friends. Don't worry, we will do you no harm.' Belle, reassured her again as she held out her hand and helped Mary to her feet. Donald took her arm. Belle walked at her other side. Duncan walked behind them.

The rain had stopped. Their feet sank into the mud, making the going hard. She felt her eyes grow heavy and her head fall forward. Then her knees bent. Strong arms lifted her up; she laid her head against a shoulder and fell into a delirious sleep where she dreamt of flames, of smoke, of creatures coming out of the earth and chasing her.

* * * * * *

'Go find your sister, keep her safe!' His mother urged as the soldiers attacked.

'But!'

'Go now. Through the window. Be quick. And don't forget your knife,' his mother said, handing it to him as he jumped out the window. 'Take an axe, anything just to be safe.' Malcolm nodded. 'Go now, find Mary,' she said in a low, urgent whisper, her mouth close to his ear.

He landed softly on the ground and glanced from side to side checking for the soldiers – whoever they were. He saw no one other than his father rushing to defend his home. At the sight of his father he hesitated, torn between helping his parents defend their home and finding Mary. 'I have to find Mary,' he whispered to himself. Crouching, trying not to trample the few vegetables that were struggling to grow in the poor soil of the garden, he took the quickest route to the gate, pausing only to grab his axe from amongst the freshly chopped firewood.

'Mary'll be in the woods,' he said to himself. He was concentrating so much on his task that he didn't notice the stick swinging towards him until it was too late to get out of the way. The blow knocked him off his feet and he dropped the axe. As he lay on his back, a hand picked up the axe and threw it into the distance.

'Hahahhaha!' his attacker laughed.

Malcolm grimaced as he recognised Graham. Graham bullied everybody. He stole the wooden swords off the younger boys, disturbed their games and caused trouble wherever he went.

Graham smiled slyly at Malcolm lying on the ground. He hated Malcolm; he was scared of him as no matter what he did, Malcolm stood up to him. He had dreamt of getting his revenge, had spent hours planning and plotting and here, in the midst of their village being attacked, he had unexpectedly got his chance.

'Whit you doing down there?' Graham stood looking disdainfully at him.

He tried to get up but Graham pushed him back down and held him there with his foot. 'Running away,' he taunted.

'Let me up.'

'No.' Graham kicked him in the ribs, doubling him up in pain. Graham raised his foot to kick him again; this time Malcolm grabbed his foot and pulled Graham down beside him. As he fell, Malcolm stood up. He was not going to let Graham get in his way. He was going to fight.

Graham scrambled to his feet, hands in fists, cursing and swearing. He lashed out at Malcolm who somehow managed to avoid being hit. Again and again Graham punched and Malcolm skipped from side to side avoiding the blows, until he saw his chance and punched Graham hard on the nose. Blood squirted everywhere. Graham stumbled forward, holding his nose and tripped over a stone, landing flat on his face.

'Are you...?' Malcolm shook his head. 'I'm sorry. I have to look for Mary.' The words were hardly out of his mouth before he started to run.

When he reached the end of the village, he peered slowly round the corner. All around him was chaos. Mounted soldiers were riding up and down through the centre of the village, hacking, slashing and cutting at anyone who resisted them. The thatched wooden houses were burning ferociously, the roaring flames red against the sky. Dogs were barking; cattle driven crazy by the flames, the noise and the heat were running in all directions. Even the old cart with its one wheel that the children played on was burning. Soldiers were in the fields trampling over the crops and setting fire to the barns. The children, led by an older girl, were running backwards and forwards from the well with buckets, trying to put out the fires.

The few houses that weren't burning were being defended by their owners. He could see his father armed with an axe fighting a soldier. There was his mother, armed with a frying pan and ladle seeing off another soldier. One of the dogs stood barking and growling at their side, the other lay motionless on the ground.

'Mother, father,' he said taking a step forward. He wanted to be with them. He wanted to help defend his home, his family, his village. After a few steps he stopped and shook his head, mumbling to himself, 'You can't! You have to find Mary...that's your duty now.' He turned towards the woods.

'What do we have here, a coward?' A hand grabbed him and spun him round. Malcolm, who was not small for his age, looked up and up, until his eyes met cold, hard eyes, belonging to a face that was equally as hard and cold.

'My sister... I have to.... .'

‘You have to come with me. That’s what you have to do.’ The man spoke with an English accent.

‘Why?’

‘We’re looking for a traitor who has dark hair, brown eyes and is your height and age. Unless, I’m mistaken – and I don’t think I am – that’s you! You helped James Douglas escape from us. King Edward hates James Douglas as much as he hates your usurping king. That’s why you have to come with me.’

Malcolm opened his mouth to speak, and then closed it. He had been going to ask how? How did this man know that he and his father had helped James Douglas? But that would be like confessing and he wouldn’t do that. He was proud of what he had done and would do it again.

He had been wakened one night by banging at the door. At first, as no one else had stirred he thought it was a dream, but as the banging continued and became more and more urgent, he decided to investigate. Taking his knife from under his bed – he always slept with his knife under his bed, so it would be close in case he needed it; he had never needed it until that night. With the knife ready in his hand he had made his way across the room. When he reached the door, he paused, the banging had stopped, but he could hear the people on the other side. Something told him they weren’t neighbours looking for help with an ill relative, or help recovering a cow that had wandered off and got trapped. Cautiously, he had opened the door, to reveal two armed men standing in the shadows.

‘Get your father!’ one of the men ordered in a low, yet commanding, voice. His companion stared slyly at Malcolm.

‘No need,’ his father’s voice came from directly behind him.

'I am -.'

'I know who you are, Jamie. Malcolm, let them in.'

He had stood aside to let the men, one of whom had a bad cut on his face, enter.

While his mother tended to the stranger's cut, the other man had quickly explained to his father that they were running from enemy soldiers and needed somewhere to hide for a day or two.

Without hesitation his father had agreed to help.

'I'll help too,' Malcolm offered, grabbing his cloak.

'No, you go back to bed,' his father ordered.

'No, there are two men to hide, only one of you. What if the soldiers come across you? You won't be able to defend yourself with your sore leg.' His father had always limped. 'I'm coming with you.' It had been the first time he had spoken disobediently to his father. He had looked, nervously, from his father to his mother waiting on their reaction. When it came it had taken him by surprise.

'Very well, son, but not a word to anyone.'

They had done it all themselves, his father and him, not told anyone. Yet this man knew. The only people, beside himself and his father, who knew; were James Douglas who he couldn't see betraying them, his mother and Mary. Neither of them would have said anything. But, Jamie's companion that night – yes, he could have betrayed them, something about him had left him with an uneasy feeling.

'It is really your father we want.' The man gave a malicious laugh as he looked at the destruction all around him, the villagers fighting desperately for their lives and homes. 'You'll do just as well,' he said smiling evilly.

'No,' Malcolm said defiantly. He had dealt with Graham and he would deal with this man if he had to. He was not going to be stopped from finding Mary.

'You have to come with me,' the man said angrily.

'No!' Malcolm clenched his fist and aimed it at the man who effortlessly knocked it aside. He came in for a second punch which again the man stopped with ease.

'You're a brave fool,' the man laughed, mockingly.

Ignoring him, Malcolm prepared to kick. Quick as a flash the man knocked his legs out from under him sending him sprawling to the ground.

The man reached down, picked him up and threw him on to a horse, before climbing up in front of him.

'What have you got there, Sir Giles?' a couple of soldiers asked as they rode by.

'A cowardly traitor,' Sir Giles laughed, digging his heels into his horse; he spurred it forward, crashing through the smoke and nearly running over a small figure that jumped out of the way at the last moment.

Chapter 2

As they reached the woods, Sir Giles abruptly turned his horse so they rode along the edge of the woods, keeping close to the trees. The horse galloped on and on. The shouts and screams, the cracking of the flames faded into the distance as they rode. Malcolm glanced over his shoulder, his family were back there, fighting to save their home and their lives if they weren't already dead. He had failed them, let them down. He hadn't found Mary. Where was she? Would he ever see her or his parents again? To take his mind off the fate of his family, he turned his attention to his own plight.

'Where are you taking me?'

'To learn the error of your ways, that's where. Somewhere you'll be amongst civilised people and learn to accept English rule.'

I'll never accept English rule, he promised himself as a castle came into view.

He had seen the castle before from a distance when he and his father passed by on their way to town for market days. The castle with all its comings and goings fascinated him; he liked watching the lords and ladies and the soldiers on their way to war. He hoped that one day, when he was a soldier he would stay in a castle. He had never imagined that his first visit to a castle would be as a captive. Now he wasn't so sure that he wanted to be in a castle. Up close the castle rose threateningly towards the sky. The walls were dark and grey with holes for windows and shooting arrows. Two towers rose above the outer wall.

The few men left to guard the castle shouted to the gatekeepers when they saw Sir Giles approach. The portcullis rose slowly, pulled by large iron chains that screeched and groaned with a sound painful to the ears. It rose slowly as if reluctant to let them enter. When it was finally raised it revealed two large wooden doors that screeched as they were opened. Finally, a gaping hole appeared in the wall.

'You lazy, useless bunch of cowards.' Sir Giles entered the castle grumbling and cursing the guards who, used to his abuse, ignored him.

The courtyard was unevenly cobbled and the horse tripped and slipped as it made its way towards a low building situated beside the back wall.

'Down.' The command was pointless as Sir Giles pulled Malcolm from the horse as he spoke.

Malcolm yelled as he hit the ground with a thump. Ignoring his yell, Sir Giles lifted him and dragged him half standing, half crouching through a wooden door and into the kitchen.

'Here's some extra help for you. Keep him until we find some use for him.' Sir Giles shoved Malcolm in front of him as he addressed the cook.

'But….!' Before the cook, a man with a round body, head and eyes had finished speaking, Sir Giles had stormed out of the kitchen, leaving him no choice but to deal with Malcolm.

'Sit down. Keep out the way.' Waving his hands, the cook indicated a stool in the corner.

Pushing his way through the men, women and children preparing various types of meat and vegetables, preparing more food than he had eaten in his lifetime, or was likely to eat, Malcolm sat down, determined to get out of the castle. He had to. He had to find Mary. He cast his eyes around the kitchen looking for a way out. The only way out was through the door to the courtyard. He looked for the cook, and smiled when he saw him occupied with preparing the meat. This was his chance.

‘You come back here!’ Startled by the cook leaping across the kitchen, he sat back down just as a boy carrying a chicken leg flashed past him.

‘I’ll see you hang from the battlements!’ The cook, too round and slow to catch the boy yelled at the door as it banged shut. He stood staring at the closed door for a few minutes then puffing turned back to the meat. He walked a few steps, then turned on his heels. ‘You, boy. Here!’ he boomed. Malcolm, praying that no one could hear his heart thumping, slid off the stool and made his way to stand in front of the cook.

‘Flagon, wine. Serve. Through that door,’ the cook wagged a finger in the direction of the door, ‘across the courtyard, in the door opposite, the Great Hall is upstairs. Now!’ The cook had barely finished talking as Malcolm grabbed the flagon, and with wine slopping over the edge ran out of the kitchen, shutting the door on the cook shouting something about spilling wine and hanging from battlements.

He stepped into the courtyard and smiled, this was his chance to escape. He listened, the only sound was the neighing of nearby horses. He looked around: nothing moved. He was alone. He stepped further into the courtyard and placing the flagon on the ground, ran to the edge of the castle wall and peered round. There were a few guards milling around the portcullis. How was he going to get past them? He could throw himself on their mercy or try and trick them. Whatever he was going to do, he would need to decide quickly.

‘What are you doing?’

He looked around but couldn’t see anyone. ‘You are hearing things now, stop it,’ he scolded himself.

‘What are you doing?’

This time he looked up, flicking his hair out of his eyes. Dread crossed his face and filled his body at the sight of an archer standing on the battlements with an arrow aimed straight at him.

'What are you doing?'

'Great hall…wine,' were the only words he could muster.

'The hall is that way.' The archer swung his arrow in the direction of the hall before swiftly returning to point it once more at Malcolm. 'I don't see any wine.'

'It's over there,' Malcolm pointed to where he had left the wine.

The archer looked hard at him for a few seconds. 'Well, take the wine. Don't keep the nobles waiting,' he said, lowering his bow.

Malcolm ran for the wine and dashed into the castle, kicking the door shut behind him. He stood with his back against the door, not just to keep the archer out but to steady his shaking hands and body. To get the image of the archer out of his head he looked at his surroundings. A long corridor with doors on each side stretched out in front of him, stairs headed up into a darkness broken by faint light and even fainter voices. To stop his hands from shaking he clasped the flagon with both hands, then made his way along the corridor and up the stairs following the sound of the voices.

At the top of the stairs he found himself standing opposite large doors from under which light shone. Loud voices came from the other side. He paused repeating to himself, 'I'm not afraid, I'm not afraid.' How could he be afraid? Wasn't he the boy who had helped James Douglas to escape?

He pushed the door open and found himself in a room ten times the size of his home. The walls hung with tapestries and heraldic shields. The floor was strewn with straw and herbs. Jugglers and acrobats danced, skipped and performed around the hall. A table, laid with silver dishes, stood raised above all others. At its centre sat a man; from his dress Malcolm figured he was the lord of the castle. At his side sat various noblemen. The lesser nobles sat at tables running off from the top table. All the men sat on wooden benches. Two dogs lay in front of the hearth. Torches, flaming brightly, hung from the walls and in stands near the table.

The lord was speaking loudly, 'King Edward is marching with a large army. The Scots will soon be taught the error of their ways. The Bruce will be dead and they will be forced to accept King Edward as their king.' The men listening to him nodded and smiled in agreement. 'Finally, I'll be able to return to England, to civilisation and be free of this backward, coarse, contemptible country whose citizens are no better than wild animals.' A couple of men sitting near the lord looked shocked. The lord seeing their expressions and hearing their sharp intake of breath continued with less sincerity. 'That does not include those Scots sitting here today, of course.' None of the men looked like they believed him.

Malcolm gritted his teeth and raised his head up. He put a smile on his face and holding his head high, as steadily as he could with shaking legs, approached the top table, telling himself he was not afraid. He made directly for the lord. He raised the flagon of wine to refill the beaker but the lord put his hand out and covered it.

'Who have we here?' he asked, looking directly at Malcolm.

Malcolm did not say a word. He was not going to tell this man anything. He was not going to speak.

'Well, who are you boy? I have not seen you serving at my table before.'

Still he remained silent.

‘Have you lost your tongue, boy?’ The lord sounded impatient and angry.

‘Excuse me, My Lord,’ a loud, confident, arrogant voice spoke.

‘What is it, Sir Giles?’

‘That is the boy I was telling you about, My Lord, the traitor I caught running away from a fight,’ Sir Giles explained

‘A coward? Are you, my boy?’ the lord sneered.

The jugglers had stopped juggling. The acrobats had stopped jumping and balancing. No one spoke. All eyes were on him.

‘I was looking for my sister,’ he explained trying to sound brave, although inside he was shaking.

Ignoring him, the lord continued, ‘A Scottish coward. I do not like cowards or Scots.' Again some of the men sitting around the table squirmed uncomfortably, laughing he continued. ‘Apart from those Scots here who do not believe in Robert Bruce’s right to be king.’ All the Scotsmen smiled and nodded indulgently at him.

Then with a mocking expression on his face he turned to Malcolm, ‘Do you want Robert Bruce or King Edward to be king of Scotland?’

Malcolm hesitated. He wanted Robert Bruce to be King but he was in a room full of men who supported King Edward. If he said Robert Bruce there was no telling what they might do.

‘I…I….I.’

‘Come on, boy spit it out.’ Sir Giles urged.

‘Robert Bruce or King Edward?’ the lord repeated.

‘Robert Bruce.’ Malcolm stammered.

‘Not only are you a coward but you are a fool too!’ As he spoke the lord pushed his tumbler towards Malcolm.

His hand shaking, Malcolm raised the flagon to fill the lord's beaker but missed and poured the wine over the table and the lord.

'Why! You.. .' The lord raised his hand as if to slap Malcolm, who dropped the flagon of wine and closed his eyes to receive the slap, but it never came.

When he opened his eyes one of the noblemen was holding the wrist of the lord.

'Do you think that is wise, my lord?' the nobleman asked. 'If you want the Scots to support you, should you not show benevolence?'

Angrily the lord stared at his questioner then growled; 'Standing up for your countrymen now are we, Sir Alexander?'

'No, standing up for a boy.' Alexander answered staring him straight in the eye.

The lord stared back then growled, 'Get the boy out of my sight.'

Malcolm ran out of the hall.

'Wait! Wait a minute.' The Scottish nobleman who had come to his aid had followed him.

'What is your name?' he asked holding out his hand. 'I am Sir Alexander. There is no need to be afraid of me. I am with the English for my own reasons. Did you run away from the fight today?'

Nervously, he shook the man's hand. 'Malcolm. No, I was looking for my sister.'

'Did you find her?'

He shook his head. 'She was in the woods when the soldiers came. I don't know where she is.'

'So, you want to get out of this place to look for her?'

'Yes.'

'I may not be able to help you escape, but I may be able to get you a position as a squire, that would get you out of the castle. Would you like that?'

Malcolm nodded.

'I will see what I can do. Now go.'

He stared blankly at Sir Alexander.

'Do you not have any where to go?'

He shook his head.

Sir Alexander looked curiously at him for a while then addressed a servant girl who was crossing the passageway.

'Send Poor John here to me immediately.'

The girl nodded and ran off.

After a few minutes the boy who had stolen the chicken leg came strolling along the corridor, licking his lips. As he approached, Malcolm was able to get a good look at him. He had tousled hair, his clothes were ragged, a leather pouch, which Malcolm soon learned he was never parted from, hung at his side. There was a smile on his face; a charming and disarming smile.

On reaching Sir Alexander he bowed before speaking. 'You sent for me sire? At your service.'

Sir Alexander laughed and lifted his hand as if to pat the boy's head but stopped himself.

'Enough of that, John,' he tried to sound commanding but the softness of his voice betrayed the friendliness.

'This is Malcolm. He is a prisoner of Sir Giles. Look after him for me.'

'Aye, Sir.'

'I will see what I can do,' Sir Alexander winked at Malcolm as he returned to the hall.

John headed up the stairs signalling to Malcolm to follow him. They climbed up and up, round and round. The higher they climbed the darker it became. Whereas the lower floors had been elaborately furnished and well lit to show their magnificence, the upper levels were poorly decorated and poorly lit to disguise the signs of neglect.

They climbed to the top of one of the towers, past the once beautifully decorated bedrooms now serving as dormitories for the garrison. Malcolm smiled to himself at how the bleakness of this part of the castle reflected his mood. Here he was a prisoner; a strange prisoner without shackles but a prisoner nonetheless. A young boy who had helped one of England's greatest enemies escape, stuck in a castle full of Englishmen. He had failed, failed his parents and failed Mary. She was out there somewhere in the rain, the rain that to him seemed to fall without a sound. He halted at the window trying to peer through the rain for any sign of movement or a small figure on the horizon; even if she were a prisoner with him it would be better than no Mary at all. Was she even alive? He wondered.

'Hurry!' John shouted over his shoulder.

For now all he could do was go where he was told and do as he was asked. He would get out of here somehow.

'We're here,' John declared as he pushed open a door at the top of the tower.

'Welcome to my room.'

The room was small and dreary. The remains of a fire lay in the hearth. A bundle of firewood sat in the corner. Cobwebs hung from the beams and the walls. The floor was covered in dirt. A rat ran in front of them.

'You can sleep there,' John pointed to a recess opposite the fire place. He handed Malcolm a couple of furs from his pile and a blanket. 'I'll light a fire. Get some warmth. We can't have a fire all the time. Firewood can be difficult to find.' He was already down on his knees poking at the fireplace adding more wood to it. Then he disappeared from the room and returned with a flaming torch and lit the fire.

'Hungry?'

Malcolm found himself unable to answer that simple question. Thoughts collided in his mind; all he could do was stand and listen to John.

When he eventually opened his mouth to speak he realised that John wasn't in the room anymore. He was still standing on the same spot when John returned and handed him a piece of bread and cheese.

'Where did you get that?' Malcolm asked.

'If I don't tell you, you can't get into trouble; that's the way it is.' John smiled mysteriously. 'Eat and rest.'

He ate, hungrily, crouched by the fire for warmth. Then lying down he fell into a disturbed sleep. He woke sweating from a dream about Mary as the last of the fire died away to nothing. The light Scottish night came in through the window illuminating a spider as it wove its web. He watched the spider work, finding it strangely comforting, as his thoughts wandered to Mary.

* * * * * *

The rain came through the gaps in the interwoven branches that formed the shelter. Figures flickered in and out, coming and going. Voices merged into one. Mary was hot, very hot. Every so often she was aware of a beaker being held to her lips and a warm liquid sliding down her throat. A hand followed by the sensation of a wet cloth on her forehead and murmurings. Her heavy eyes would close until the sound of her scream that came distant and piercing wakened her.

How long she lay until the figures gained faces and the voices separated from each other, she did not know. For a while she lay still, then with a great effort she tried to move her sore, aching body away from the puddles that lay all around but failed. Slowly, steadily, her head swimming, she took in her surroundings. She was lying on furs, covered by cloaks, under a canopy made by the entwined branches of nearby trees; the canopy was at its thickest above her. A group of weather beaten, grubby men, some scarred and cut, some wearing leather brigandines, others with cloaks pulled tightly around them, huddled together for warmth. The two men from the forest were lighting a fire.

'I'm glad the rain's stopped,' one of the men sitting huddled together said.

'Aye! Me too.'

'How long's it been?'

'Three days. Three days of rain. Three days in which the English sat cosy and warm in our castles, while we sat freezing here.'

'Aye, but they'll no be there for long,' the first man laughed as he stood up to shake and wring the water from his cloak.

All the men nodded or shouted their agreement.

'Whit do you say, Jamie?' He addressed a dark-haired, swarthy man sitting near him. 'Enough sitting time for action.'

'You're awake.' Jamie's reply was drowned out by Belle, sounding relieved, as she appeared by her side. 'We were getting worried. You've been ill for days. The rain has finally stopped. Come and sit by the fire.'

With Belle's help Mary slowly raised herself into a sitting position. Her head hurt. She rested for a while before trying to stand up. Her legs shook and gave way from under her.

'Here, let me help you.' The man called Jamie knelt down beside her and lifted her up. 'We'll get you comfortable by the fire and find you something to eat. Duncan, can you see to that?'

Duncan produced some oats from a pouch, added water to them and cooked the mixture over the fire.

'It's not the best food for you but it is a' we 'ave,' he apologised, handing her a dry biscuit.

The first bite slid with difficulty down her throat but her stomach gratefully received it. With each bite eating became easier and she felt stronger.

'I'm Jamie Douglas,' the dark haired man introduced himself as he sat beside her. 'These are my men. All loyal to The Bruce and Scotland. The wood has been our base recently while we learn news of the English army. You are?'

'Mary.' As she looked up she caught the man's eyes, holding them for a couple of seconds, his face triggering a vague memory. She had seen him somewhere before, with the same concerned look on his face but couldn't remember where.

'Pleased to meet you. What were you doing in the woods?'

'I....' Her voice shook and her eyes filled with tears; she hadn't thought about her family until now. She could be all alone in the world. What would become of her? Who would look after her? Her only relative was her father's brother, who worked for some nobleman. She had never met him but Malcolm had. She had questioned him about their uncle.

'He's just like father.' was all he would say.

Just like father, that was good. Maybe she could live with him. If she couldn't, she would spend her days begging if she did not die in this war.

'I don't know if my family are dead or alive.' The tears rolled down her face. 'My village was burned. I was in the woods at the time - when I got to the village there was nothing but smoke and flames. I couldn't see anyone or anything apart from shadows. I got scared and ran. I don't know what happened!'

Jamie sat patiently waiting for her to stop crying.

'Your village has been totally destroyed.' Jamie spoke softly. 'The only signs of life are the wild animals nosing about in the remains.'

'Why? Who?' she asked through the tears.

'English soldiers more than likely. There's a garrison near here. They are preparing for the upcoming battle.'

'By destroying my home? Burning my village? Killing my family?'

'To put fear into the people so they won't support King Robert. Your village being destroyed doesn't mean that your family are dead. They could have disappeared into the hills for safety. They could be anywhere.' He tried to comfort her. 'I promise that I will help you find your family.' For some time he stared at the dancing flames then continued, 'I received unsettling news today which means we have to move from here. You are too weak to come with us. We can not take you home and we can not leave you in the woods. What to do with you?' Jamie sat silently.

'Whit aboot Ol' Jock?' Donald suggested.

'That's it, Donald, we will take her to Old Jock. He'll take care of her for us. Mary, do you feel up to travelling a short distance?'

She nodded.

'Good, Belle, you take her on your horse. Duncan, you see to the fire. Donald, you lift Mary on to Belle's horse. We will need to go slowly.'

Jamie blew his horn and within minutes men appeared from amongst the trees and mounted their horses. For a split second his brow darkened at two of the men but he merely shook his head and continued on his way.

Chapter 3

After a slow ride, during which she had to use all her strength to keep from falling from Belle's horse, they arrived at a tumbledown cottage, partially hidden behind bushes. Jamie dismounted and lifted her from Belle's horse. 'Belle, you stay with me. Duncan and Donald, keep watch. We'll all meet at the old barn,' Jamie ordered as the rest of the men nodded and rode off.

Without knocking or announcing their presence, they entered the cottage. An old man was sitting by the fire.

'Who's there?'

'A friend, Jock' Jamie replied.

'All friends are welcome in the name of King Robert.'

'Good,' Jamie laughed as the old man came to greet them.

'Jamie, my lad it is good to see you. How are you?' Jock stopped when he noticed Mary in Jamie's arms. 'Who's this?' He moved over to the bed standing in the corner, 'She needs rest,' he said knowingly.

'Can you keep her, Jock? We have work to do.'

Jock shook his head, 'Only for a few days. I have to go into England on an errand for King Robert.'

Jamie stooped to put Mary to bed. What was he to do? He couldn't abandon her. She was under his protection now. Old Jock's would be the safest place for her but if Jock was going away?

Before speaking he looked at Belle, then Mary; he only had one option.

'Could you bring her to us at the old barn on your way over the border?'

'Yes. But Jamie, who is she?'

‘Her name is Mary. I owe my life to her father, it is because of me her home was burnt and her family destroyed.’

Once Jamie and Belle had left, Jock disappeared outside returning with his hands full of what could have been weeds. He chopped, he ground, he boiled and handed Mary the results to drink

She drank, ‘Yuck. What is it?’

‘My secret recipe, it’ll make you better! Now drink it.’ Jock instructed.

Almost as soon as she had finished drinking she fell asleep.

The next morning, she lay watching Jock move around the bare cottage; besides the bed, there were two chairs by the fire, a table and an old chest. A cloak hung on a hook on the wall, a staff stood beside the door.

‘I‘m Mary,’ she introduced herself as Old Jock came to check on her.

‘I know. How do you feel?’

‘Better, but my head hurts.’

‘You are looking better than you were last night when you were brought here.’ Old Jock crossed to the fire and stirred the contents of a pot as he talked. Then taking a couple of bowls from the shelf he handed her a bowl of porridge.

‘That’ll build your strength up.’

He was right, as later that day she felt strong enough to accompany him when he went to fetch water from a nearby stream.

As she knelt down to drink from the stream, she caught a glimpse of her reflection in the water. Her cheeks, usually rosy under the dirt of misadventures were now pale; her hair hung lank and limp. The old brown tunic that Jock had given her, in place of her own clothes that had been destroyed by the mud and rain, made her look like a beggar. She stared at her image for a while, then took a drink. The water felt cold and fresh. She drank some more. Then cupping her hands together, she threw water over her face. The cold water felt good and as she drank she felt more like herself. A shiver ran through her body; not from the water but from a sense that she was not alone. Old Jock was nearby leaning on his staff staring into space. Yet she could feel eyes looking hard at her, feel them boring in to her back. She looked around; there was no one there. Still she could feel someone watching her. As she stood up a movement amongst the trees caught her eyes.

'Who's there?' she asked loudly.

'Ssshh!' Jock grabbed her shoulder. 'Let's go.' They headed off at a steady speed.

'Who do you think was watching us?' she asked.

'I don't know. There are so many enemies around, both Scottish and English. You never really know who is friend or foe.'

As they moved away a man turned and headed back into the woods, an evil smile on his face.

'Is that the girl?' he asked the two men waiting restlessly nearby.

They nodded.

'You want them both – dead?'

They nodded, 'Dead, that'll finish Jamie – the old man and the girl dead.' They both laughed.

'Kill a child?' Tom shuddered, 'I'm not sure I could do that.'

'You don't have to kill her, just get her out the way. Somewhere she won't be seen or heard 'til all is over.'

'All is over?' Tom scrunched his eyebrows, questioningly.

‘Until England rules Scotland and Jamie and King Robert are dead and we three get the power and status we deserve.’ They laughed.

Tom nodded, the cruel smile returning to his face.

‘Talking of Jamie..?’ the man nearest to Tom said.

‘Aye, Walter we had better get back tae him.’ His companion answered the unfinished question as they disappeared among the trees leaving Tom alone.

The next morning Mary helped Jock sweep the floors and prepare for his journey.

‘Can I go for a walk?’ she asked when they had finished. She liked Old Jock, he was kind and told interesting stories. But she was bored being stuck in doors.

‘Yes but be careful.’

‘I will,’ she promised.

‘Don’t go too far away from the house,’ Jock shouted after her.

She ran outside, jumping and skipping. It was a beautiful summer’s day. A slight breeze cooled the heat of the sun. She spun round. She ran her hands over the tree trunks and talked to herself or spoke softly to the flowers. She picked and ate wild berries. She imagined that her dress was the colour of the summer sky catching the breeze as she danced and skipped around an orchard.

She stopped dreaming when the light around her darkened and a figure appeared in front of her. A figure with a crooked nose, lopsided eyes, a mouth turning up at one side and down at the other. A figure whose eyes bored into her before he reached out to grab her. Just in time she dodged out the way and turned on her heels. She ran towards Jock’s cottage. The man followed her. She glanced over her shoulder; he was still following her. She ran faster. Again, she looked over her shoulder. He was gaining on her. She ran as fast as she could. Suddenly she realised that she could not hear footsteps behind her or the heavy breathing of the man. She looked over her shoulder; the man was still running; but in the opposite direction.

Just as she was puzzling over why the man had changed direction she was startled, by a noise from behind. She spun round and froze.

Her head spun as she found herself back in the woods, running in all directions, not knowing where to go. She was surrounded by smoke and the cracking of flames, large dark shadows were thundering towards her. A scream rose in her throat but as her lips wouldn't move it came to nothing. The demons came on swiftly. She wanted to run but couldn't; her legs stuck to the ground. An image of her family lying dead popped into her head. 'Mother, Father, Malcolm,' she whispered falling to her knees, frightened, she waited for the demons to reach her. At the last moment, the demons separated and one charged off in the direction of the running man, the other demon pulled up beside her.

'Are you hurt?' the voice sounded caring and worried.

She looked up, there was no smoke, no demon, only a man and a horse.

'Were you heading to Old Jock's?' he asked, dismounting and helping her to stand.

She nodded.

'Then we'll accompany you. Make sure you get there safely.' Leading his horse with one hand and holding Mary's hand in the other, they made their way back to Old Jock's. The other rider, having failed to catch the running man caught up with them.

Old Jock was watching for them as they approached. 'Mary, where did you go? I told you not to go far from the house,' he scolded her.

'I'm sorry.'

'Don't scold her so Jock. She has had a scare,' her rescuer explained.

'What happened?'

Quickly, her rescuer told Jock how he and his companion had come across Mary being chased by a man.

'Well, you will be safe in here.' Jock stood aside to let Mary and her rescuer enter; the other man waited outside.

They sat by the ever present fire. Jock claimed that he always felt cold even in the height of summer.

Mary sat on the floor, her knees pulled up to her chin, and listened to their conversation, looking from one to the other as they spoke. The new arrival had shoulder length wavy brown hair. His unshaven face was haggard and rugged.

He was dressed like a soldier. His trousers were not only ripped and torn but covered in grass and dirt, his chainmail shirt was splattered in mud. A dagger and an axe hung from a belt around his waist. Yet, despite his appearance, something about him made her feel he was important.

Jock and the stranger talked together about the current conflict and the upcoming battle that could free Scotland or leave her forever shackled to England.

The conversation drifted into the background as in her mind, Mary was transported back to a different hearth. She was sitting at the feet of her mother who was spinning the wool that would eventually be made into their clothes or sold. Malcolm, lost in thought, allowed the bowl he was carving to fall to the floor and her father was singing songs and telling tales of heroes old and new.

'What's the matter?' Old Jock sounded concerned; her reverie disturbed, Mary looked at him through the tears that had begun to fall down her face.

'I hate this war. It has killed my family, destroyed my home. My family are dead. Why does it matter who rules? Why can King Robert not let King Edward rule Scotland if it will stop the fighting? My family are dead because of King Robert,' she shouted through the tears.

'This war - ' The stranger paused and Mary was surprised to see tears in the eyes of a man who looked like he led a hard life of fighting, his voice shook as he continued. 'This war has killed my brothers and my wife and daughter are captives in England. There has been many a time when I could have given up. But I can't.. .' his voice trailed off.

'Who are you?' Mary asked, ashamed of her outburst.

'I am Robert Bruce.'

'King Robert?'

'Yes.'

'But, you don't look like a king,' she spluttered out, embarrassed.

'What does a king look like?' King Robert asked, a faint twinkle in his eyes.

'He should wear a crown and live in a castle. He would eat banquets.'

'The forest and hills of Scotland are my castles. I wear a helmet to protect myself from sword blows, instead of a crown. My food is the wild berries, the deer,' he said

'I'm sorry.' Mary curtsied, ashamed.

'There is no need. There is no need.' Robert Bruce patted her on the shoulder before addressing Old Jock.

‘I must leave now, Jock. Good luck with your journey.' He grabbed Jock’s thin hands between his two hands, holding them for a few moments. ‘Goodbye.’

Mary stood at the door watching as King Robert and his companion rode off.

Next morning, the sun hadn’t long risen when Old Jock, with bread in a bag slung over his shoulder, staff in hand and Mary with a cloak pulled round her shoulders, set off to meet up with Jamie.

As they skirted the edge of the woods, the leaves rustling in the wind, the sound of hurried footsteps came from behind the trees.

‘Hurry, Mary,’ Jock urged too late as a man jumped out in front of them.

'Give me your money, your goods,’ he demanded, threatening Jock with a dagger.

‘Tom Comyn, what are you up to?’

‘Give me your money, your goods,’ Tom repeated.

‘Last I heard you were over the border helping the English; working with them to defeat Scotland. You’ll be here spying for them more than likely. Are they not paying you enough that you have to go robbing?’ Jock ignored Tom’s demand for money.

‘I am working with the English, not to beat Scotland but to defeat the murderer Bruce, who killed my kinsman. The Comyns should rule in Scotland not the Bruces.' His voice shook with hate.

‘Robert Bruce is King of Scots, you can’t change that.’

‘Maybe not but the English can and will.’

‘I wouldn’t be so sure of that.’

‘You Bruce supporters are so arrogant. How do you, with only peasants and outlaws, expect to beat the greatest, most powerful army in the world?’ Tom sneered.

'The greatest, most powerful army in the world was beaten once before at Stirling Bridge by peasants and outlaws.'

'That outlaw Wallace was lucky! Surely the defeat at Falkirk showed that?'

'This war has shown us many things, mainly who the traitors to Scotland are,' Jock declared.

'I am no traitor to Scotland, just to Robert Bruce.'

'That is the same thing. I don't have time to stand here discussing the issue with you. Come, Mary.' Jock held out his hand to her.

With one movement Tom leapt forward and stabbed at Jock with his dagger. Jock lifted his staff up and brought it down hard on Tom's hand making him drop the dagger. He brought the other end up and round, hitting Tom hard on the side and knocking him over.

Mary stood in the shadows watching, planning what to do if Jock was killed or injured, what was the best way to escape and where to go? She would have to help Jock if he was injured, she couldn't leave him behind. Her thoughts were disturbed by a scream; after a few failed attempts Tom had managed to stand up again.

'Just the old man, just Old Jock. I will kill him, not the lassie. I can't kill a lassie. I'll take her to…to my aunt's in Edinburgh; she'll keep the lass for me, until this is over,' Tom thought as he rose to his feet. His dagger gone, he pulled out an axe and lunged once more at Old Jock, who stepped aside. Tom ran straight past him, nearly hitting a tree. Red faced and angry, he stopped and turning headed towards Jock again, the axe held above his head. As he passed Mary, she stuck her foot out and tripped him up, sending him flying face first on to the ground, his axe sinking into the mud. He reached for the axe but Mary had got to it first and was swinging it in front of her. Tom tried to grab her but couldn't get past the axe.

'Why you little…. ,' Tom yelled, scrambling to his feet and running off.

'You can certainly take care of yourself,' Jock laughed.

She handed him the axe. Jock shook his head. 'You keep it.'

She smiled in thanks. 'That's the man who chased me yesterday.'

Jock nodded. 'Word has got out that you are under the protection of James Douglas. They know he protects his friends. They can use you to get at him. Trap him. Kill him and therefore destroy one of their greatest enemies. Though, how the likes of Tom Comyn would know your connection to Jamie beats me.'

Mary shuddered.

'Don't worry. You'll be safe. Nothing will happen to you,' Jock reassured her as he marched off so fast that she struggled to keep up with him.

Without any further trouble they arrived at a desolate barn; beside it was the burnt out remains of a cottage, the fields all around had been burnt and all the crops destroyed. The barn had lost part of one wall and only half the roof remained.

'Aaaaa!' Mary screamed as two men appeared as if from nowhere, with swords drawn.

'Oh, it's yoursel', Jock.'

'Hello, lass, didnae mean to scare you.' With that the men disappeared back into the shadows.

As they approached the barn two other men, one with a recent scar on his face, came round the corner returning from guard duty. They stared open mouthed and wide eyed at Old Jock and Mary, their eyes darting quickly from one to the other.

‘What’s the matter?’ Jock asked.

‘Eh! Eh! Eh!....’

The man with the scarred face recovered first. ‘We are surprised to see you both so soon. That’s all,’ he said practically running into the barn.

‘We heard a scream,’ Jamie said as they entered, behind the men.

‘Mary was scared by your guards appearing unexpectedly,’ Jock explained.

‘I’m sorry you were scared by my guards, you can’t be too careful these days. It’s good to see you, Jock and you, Mary, glad you are looking well.’ Jamie greeted them cheerily, as the men, the alarm over, retook their seats around the fire which was under the only remaining part of the roof or curled up on the stack of hay to sleep. All except the man with the scarred face and his companion, who stood whispering in the corner.

‘Come sit by the fire. Rest awhile,’ Jamie continued.

‘You too, Mary,’ Belle beckoned her over to sit beside her and the twins. As she sat down all the men smiled at her or greeted her cheerily.

‘I can’t stay, Jamie,’ Jock said.

‘Are you sure, Jock?’

‘Yes, I‘ve lost enough time as it is. We were attacked by Tom Comyn on the way here.’

‘Tom Comyn? I thought he was in England.’

‘So did I, he is back causing trouble here.’

‘The Comyns will always cause trouble. They will never accept Robert Bruce as king. Tom is sly and cowardly.’

‘But dangerous with it,’ Jock butted in.

‘They need to be dealt with.' The tone of Jamie’s voice made Mary shiver. ‘Jock, if you will not stay. I will lend you a couple of men to escort you to the border.'

'There is no need.'

'There is every need. You have been attacked once today.' Jamie spoke with authority. 'Duncan, Donald, make sure Jock gets safely to the border,' he ordered. 'Go no further and be back before noon in two days, be quick.'

'Aye, Jamie.'

'Bye, Mary.' Jock turned and waved as he left.

'Bye, Jock. Will...' She was going to ask if she would see him again but he had left before she had finished.

Whilst, they waited for the Campbell twins to return, the men raided or attacked the English who lived nearby or the Scots who were in the pay of the English, or hunted for food.

'Why are you attacking the English who haven't done anything wrong?' Mary asked Belle, one morning after she had returned from one of the raids.

'To prevent them from helping the English army when it arrives.'

'But they haven't done anything wrong?'

'It is true, Mary that not all of the English people living in Scotland are our enemies. Unfortunately, we can not risk them being able to help the English army.'

'If they are living here, why would they want to join the English army? Surely they would want to help us?'

Belle laughed, 'Things don't work like that, Mary. They could be forced to help the English army – even if they didn't want to. Now be quiet, let me rest then I will show you how to use that axe of yours.'

'Duncan and Donald should have been back before now,' Hugh, as the man with the scarred face was called, suggested. It was late in the afternoon of the second day and the men were becoming restless.

'They should have been back at noon.' Jamie agreed.

'So why we waiting on them?'

'They are two of my best men I can't...don't want to leave without them.'

Hugh continued, catching the eyes of Walter who was standing nearby, 'They'll have found whisky and be lying in a ditch somewhere.' That'll cause them trouble, he smirked to himself, then maybe Jamie will get rid of them, with them about it is too dangerous. They are always watching Walter and me. They are too loyal to darling Jamie and will do anything for him.

'They wouldn't be drunk. Not now.' Jamie sounded confident.

'How can you be so sure? They're highlanders after all,' Hugh continued, stirring.

'Cause they are loyal to Bruce and myself, that is why I know they will not be drunk. If they are delayed they will have good reason for being so.'

Hugh's heart sank. It would take more than an accusation of drunkenness to get Jamie to turn against the twins. It would be hard, but they – him and Walter would find a way to destroy Jamie and his band of men. They would be rich under English rule, paid handsomely for the body of Jamie Douglas.

'What if they don't come back?' Walter helped Hugh out.

'They will.'

'You seem sure, what if they don't?'

Jamie pondered for a while, not only were the twins his best and most loyal men but they were also his friends. He didn't want to leave them behind, especially if they were injured or in need of his help.

But loyalty to Scotland had to come before loyalty to friends, 'We'll give them 'til sundown. If they haven't returned by then we'll leave without them.'

'You can't leave them behind!' Belle sounded horrified.

'Aye, what would you do with out Duncan and Donald,' Walter teased her.

As Belle flushed a sparkle that could have been anger shone in her eyes.

''Til sunrise tomorrow. That is the latest, Belle. I promise. We will wait 'til then, no longer.' Jamie sounded worried as he turned his back and walked a little distance away where he stood staring into the distance as if willing Duncan and Donald to appear on the horizon.

'Why do we have to leave?'

'You do ask a lot of questions, Mary.' Belle sounded exasperated.

'Are you angry with me?'

A weak smile appeared on Belle's face. 'No, Mary I'm not angry. I'm worried about Duncan and Donald; it's not like them not to return.'

'I'm worried too. I don't want them to be hurt.'

'Neither do I.'

'So, why can we not wait for them, or go looking for them?'

'Cause it is too dangerous; hiding in the forest and attacking at night, or when we have the element of surprise is one thing. But we can't risk being in one place too long in case some of the English spies spot us and report our position. There has been a lot of activity around the forest and not all of it ours,' Belle said mysteriously. 'That's why we can't wait too long for the twins.'

* * * * * *

The days had been a blur, Malcolm didn't know if he had been in the castle one day or one week. Since his capture he had spent every day with John, avoiding Sir Giles and the other nobles, or watching the nobles setting out and returning from hunting or counting how many soldiers set out to fight the Scots and how many returned. There had been a few days of torrential rain, when no-one had left the castle; those days had dragged.

'Hello, young Malcolm.' He was standing with John having just returned from watching another group of soldiers leave to hunt down the Scots when Sir Alexander greeted him. 'Did John get you sorted?'

'Aye, I did sir,' John answered instead of Malcolm.

'Good, I'm glad to hear it. Be careful, all the talk this past week has been about you the boy who helped James Douglas to escape and who threw wine over the lord. Not everyone is laughing mind,' Sir Alexander warned. 'I don't think that they'll do you any harm, but you can't be too careful. Stay with John, he'll look after you.' With that Sir Alexander walked off.

'Why is Sir Alexander with the English?' Malcolm asked

'He is related to the King of England. His brother is with the Scots,' John said laughing as Malcolm looked confused. 'Sir Alexander's mother is aunt to King Edward, his father is Scottish. When war broke out between the two countries, they felt it best if one brother supported the Scots and the other the English. Keep everyone happy. Sir Alexander got the tough end of the bargain; that is the way it is.'

'Did you get the tough end of a bargain too?' Malcolm had been curious about John for a while. They had been all over the castle together, searching for a way to escape; or at least he had. John had been through every corner of the castle before. He knew where everything was and knew everything about everybody - even the nobles. John had tried to persuade him to go into the nobles' rooms but, still reeling from his run in with Sir Giles and the lord, he had refused. To keep John happy and to quench his curiosity he had peered into the rooms through their partially open doors. The only time he had been near the nobles was when John had dragged him into the Great Hall when the nobles were feasting, while John mingled with the nobles; relieving them of some of their riches as he did so. He had stood, his back to the wall and close to the door, watching.

Afterwards, he had asked John the question, he desperately wanted to know the answer to, had the lord given the orders to attack his village?

John had merely laughed, 'Nobody listens to him - they tolerate him because of his title. If anyone had given the orders to attack your village it would've been Sir Giles.' On hearing that he promised himself that he would get revenge on Sir Giles.

'I hate them!'

'Hate who?' Malcolm asked taken aback by John's outburst.

'I hate the nobles. That is why I'm with them, that is why I steal from them; that is the way it is.' He stared, intently, at Malcolm for a few minutes as if deciding whether to trust him or not, before continuing. 'My father was King Edward's friend, not the fool we have now but his father. One day he decided that my father was no longer a friend. Why I don't know. He destroyed my father and had him executed. Sir Giles and his friends, most of the noblemen in the castle, helped King Edward destroy my father. I swore that I would make them pay. They do not deserve their riches. That is why I steal from them. They are all fools, apart from Sir Alexander who is a friend. What they don't know is that my father, always a cautious man, knew King Edward could be dangerous, he hid money away in case we needed it. He told me where the money is hidden. I am going to get out of here and find it - that is the way it is.' John stopped for breath.

'How are you going to get out of here?'

'Why do you want to know?' John said a hint of suspicion suddenly appearing in his voice.

'I want to get out of here too. I need to find my sister.'

'Why didn't you say something earlier?' The smile covered the whole of John's face. 'You want the small kitchen, it leads to a quiet part of the courtyard and is hidden from the battlements.'

Malcolm kicked himself, he had forgotten about the door in the kitchen that lead to a smaller kitchen; for use when the main kitchen was running at full capacity. The roof of this building butted up against the back wall and would hide someone from view. But how to escape? The only entrance to the castle was the portcullis; the kitchens were at the other side of the castle. He would need to get from the kitchen to the portcullis. Then past the guards, not only the ones on the portcullis but also the ones on the battlements who would see him once he was outside

'Where do I go from there?'

'I can't tell you that.' John looked like he wanted to say more, but was prevented from doing so by the sound of footsteps approaching.

'Did the nobles get their wine then?' The archer who had threatened him appeared at his side.

'Yes,' Malcolm said, his eyes falling to the bow in the archer's hand and the arrows hanging on his back.

'Have you ever used a bow before?' The archer smiled at Malcolm's curiosity.

Malcolm shook his head.

'Come then, I will show you.'

They headed to the corner of the courtyard, where the archers practised. At first, he struggled to pull the bow back to his ear, but after some tuition from Simon, he succeeded. As arrow after arrow hit the target he pictured them driving into Sir Giles; he could use the arrows to get out of the castle; he would take the bow with him and if he was challenged defend himself. He was after all, the boy who helped James Douglas to escape, who would stand up to him?

'Malcolm, Malcolm.' Simon tapped him on the shoulder. 'You're in a world of your own. I have to get back on duty now. Why don't you come with me to the battlements?'

He jumped at the chance. From the battlements he would get a view of the surrounding countryside and be able to work out his escape route.

Chapter 4

Malcolm had spent most of the past few days either here behind the kitchen or on the battlements. His initial excitement at being on the battlements had turned to disappointment. The countryside all around the castle was either naturally flat or had been burnt by one side then the other in their attempts to gain supremacy. Once outside the castle there would be nowhere for him to hide, no trees or bushes that he could use for cover. He would need to come up with an escape plan that accounted for this.

Despite his disappointment he spent a lot of time on the battlements. Amongst the garrison he was with his own type, the peasants and farmers who were also soldiers. He had always looked forward with excitement to being a soldier, of travelling the country or even going overseas to fight in the crusades. Now soldiering didn't look quite so appealing. To begin with, the soldiers in the garrison were all gaunt and half-starved, surviving on a diet of grains, oats and ale. They never left the castle, unless it was to attack the enemy. He had asked them about York and the other towns they had marched through on their way to Scotland; they could tell him about the women and the drinking but nothing else.

He wouldn't have anything to tell Mary when he saw her again. He had decided she was alive; for no other reason than it made him feel better. He would find her and his parents and he would be a soldier, as it was his duty. He would live in conditions like this or worse, with very little to eat - but he would survive.

'Mary, Mary!'

'Hahahaha!'

At the sound of his sister's name, he looked up from planning his escape; Mary alive and in the castle.

He didn't stop to wonder how she came to be there but ran as fast as he could towards her. He halted disappointed and kicking himself for being a fool when he realised it was one of the kitchen maids being chased by a page.

As he headed back his attention was caught by soldiers returning from yet another attack on the Scottish rebels. The soldiers had barely stepped through the portcullis when Sir Giles came storming out of the castle.

'Where is he? Where is James Douglas?' he screamed.

The soldiers looked at each other then at the ground.

'You failed, you are useless. Why can you not catch Jamie Douglas, he is merely a man,' Sir Giles ranted. 'If I can't trust you do to a simple task like catch a Scottish rebel, I suppose I will have to do it myself. Now get out of my sight.' He watched, mumbling about useless cowardly soldiers who couldn't carry out the simplest of task as the soldiers their heads down made their way to the guardroom. As the last of the soldiers disappeared into the guardroom, he spotted Malcolm.

'Boy, boy! Wait.' He strode over the courtyard towards Malcolm.

As Sir Giles reached him Malcolm grimaced at the smell of fresh sweat, at the heat still radiating from Sir Giles' face although his anger had somewhat abated.

'So you want to be a squire?' Sir Giles spat as he spoke.

Malcolm tried to avoid the cruel, callous eyes that were staring into his. He was confused. Why did Sir Giles think he wanted to be a squire? Then he remembered that Sir Alexander had said something about finding him a position as a squire.

'I need a squire.'

Was Sir Giles asking him to be his squire? It sounded more like he was making a statement than asking a question. Could he? Could he be squire to the man responsible for burning his village? The man responsible for the death of his parents – if they were dead. The man responsible for Mary being out there alone, maybe injured, maybe suffering. But then being a squire, even to Sir Giles, would get him out of the castle and maybe provide him with a way of escaping.

'Answer me, boy,' Sir Giles spat.

'Yes,' he made up his mind.

'Fetch my horse. I will meet you here in half and hour.' Those were all the orders he got before Sir Giles vanished in to the castle.

With the back of his hand, Malcolm wiped the spit off his face as he tried to make sense of what had just happened.

'You'd better hurry.' John who had come to see what all the shouting was about urged.

'UUUhhh…. Hurry where?'

'To get Sir Giles' horse. He won't wait,'

'Sir Giles' horse?'

'Do you know which horse is Sir Giles'?' John asked.

Malcolm shook his head.

'Come, I'll help you.'

Together they headed to the stables and after questioning one of the stable boys saddled Sir Giles' horse and another one for Malcolm to ride.

'Wait with the horses for me,' Malcolm shouted over his shoulder to John.

'Why?'

He didn't get an answer as Malcolm disappeared into the tower returning, breathless, a few minutes later carrying his bow and arrows.

Malcolm was waiting with the other squires when Sir Giles and Sir Alexander arrived along with a third man who he did not recognise. They mounted their horses and waited for the others.

'Are we going far out into the forest, Giles?' the third man asked.

'Why, are you scared, Henry?'

'I don't like straying too far from the castle. The forest is the ideal place for the Scots to be hiding. I hate the way they appear, attack and leave before we even know what is happening. Especially when James Douglas leads them,' he said trembling. As he spoke his eyes darted around the castle as if he expected an entire army of Scots to come through its walls. The only Scot he could see was Sir Alexander, 'Wait until we meet them on the battlefield. Then it will be a different story.'

Both he and Sir Giles laughed.

'So you are a squire now, young Malcolm. I wanted you to be my squire but Sir Giles insisted that as he was the one who captured you that you were to be his squire. No matter, at least it gets you out of the castle. I will do what I can to help you,' Sir Alexander winked as he finished speaking.

'Conspiring with your fellow Scot are we, Sir Alexander?' Sir Giles accused.

'I was explaining that I had asked for Malcolm to be my squire but you being a far more important nobleman chose him for yourself and rightly so.' Although Sir Alexander spoke with subservience his voice had a hint of sarcasm in it.

Sir Giles laughed uncertainly. 'Well said, Sir Alexander, I am a far more important nobleman than you. I therefore get to choose my own servants and when we beat Scotland into submission I will get my pick of the land too.'

By this time all the nobles and the soldiers who formed the hunting party had joined them.

'Let's go.' Sir Giles spurred his horse through the portcullis, as soon as they were on the other side it was lowered behind them.

With the soldiers keeping back they headed off in search of deer. After about half an hour just as they reached a point where the path forked off to the left, Henry who was leading signalled for them to be quiet.

'Over there.' He pointed to where a deer could be seen standing amongst the trees. Raising his bow, he drew back the string and shot the arrow which went flying over the head of the deer, missing its target by miles. The deer ran off.

Sir Giles laughed, 'You were never very good with a bow and arrow, Henry. My blind old mother can shoot better than that.'

Henry reddened. 'If your mother is that good maybe you should get her to fight the Scots. I am sure she could do a better job than the commanders we have.'

'That is treasonable talk.' Sir Giles' voice was threatening.

'You had better go and look for your arrow, Henry,' Alexander advised trying to calm tempers.

'You are right there, Sir Alexander, one less arrow means one less dead Scotsman. It is the only way of dealing with them. Wait Henry, let Malcolm here go and look for your arrow,' Sir Giles suggested. 'On you go, boy.'

Malcolm dismounted then hesitated at the edge of the forest glancing quickly around him.

'Oh and Malcolm, in case you are thinking this is an opportunity to escape, remember this.' Sir Giles raised his bow and arrow. 'I'm a far better shot than

Henry and if I did miss, the soldiers here would quickly run you down.'

Malcolm nodded.

'Now go and fetch the arrow.'

He headed into the woods at the spot the arrow had entered and scanned the undergrowth; there was no sign of the arrow. He moved further in. With every step he moved deeper into the trees. His head turning from side to side, searching for the arrow, he caught a glimpse of Sir Giles through the trees.

'I reckon I could,' he mumbled to himself. 'I am not an expert archer but I am better than Sir Henry.' And wasn't it only this morning that Simon had explained to him how to shoot above his head? He could kill Sir Giles. If he succeeded he would be free and if he didn't surely it would cause enough confusion to allow him to escape? The soldiers wouldn't chase him, they were his friends and wasn't he the boy who had helped James Douglas to escape? He readied an arrow.

'Dinnae do it, son.' The voice came from the ground.

'What? Who are you?' Startled, he spun round looking for the person who had spoken and noticed the men half hidden by a fallen tree.

'Dinnae do it. It's too dangerous,' Donald repeated.

'Too dangerous? It would give me a chance to escape.'

'It's too dangerous.'

'He burnt my village and destroyed my family. He deserves to die!' Malcolm said passionately.

'They would run you doon.' As the man spoke he flashed a glance at his companion, who returned the glance and nodded, before returning his attention back to Malcolm.

'They wouldn't, the soldiers are my friends.'

'Friend or foe, they are soldiers and will do what they're ordered tae.'

The soldiers would run him down, do their duty; of course they would, that is what he would do. Why hadn't he thought about that?

'Malcolm, where are you?' Sir Giles shouted.

'Even if you did get awa', they would hunt you doon as a murderer.'

The man was right; he had been so busy thinking about the here and now that he hadn't thought about the consequences.

'Malcolm, do I have to come and find you?' Sir Giles sounded angry.

'I could come with you?'

'How many is there, son?'

'About thirty.'

'That is too many, there is only twa of us.'

'Malcolm, I am sending in the soldiers.'

'You'd better go.'

Malcolm turned back towards Sir Giles.

'Before, you go, can you distract them so we can get awa'?' Donald asked him.

Malcolm nodded.

'One mair thing – dinnae forget your arrow,' Duncan said handing it to him.

'I'm coming,' Malcolm shouted to appease Sir Giles.

'Where have you been?' Sir Giles demanded as soon as he came into sight.

Whoever the men were, whatever the meaning behind the furtive glance, he felt he should help them. Not only that he agreed with them; he couldn't kill Sir Giles now. But he wasn't going to let that man intimidate him.

'I had to go deep into the forest to find the arrow,' he said waving it in the air. Sir Giles stared suspiciously at him for a long time. 'Get back on your horse.'

As he mounted under Sir Giles' stare, his mind raced. How was he going to distract the hunting party long enough to let the men get away. As he settled into the saddle an idea occurred to him.

'Stop!' he yelled. Sir Giles stared at him.

'What?'

'A stag. I saw a stag down there,' he pointed down the fork of the path.

'Are you sure?'

He nodded. He hadn't seen a stag but that path would take them away from this spot, away from the men hiding in the forest.

Sir Giles wheeled his horse round violently and set off down the left path.

* * * * * *

Duncan and Donald lay unmoving until the sound of horses and the hunting party had died down. Slowly, rising to their feet, they shook the leaves and twigs and other debris off their clothes.

'Hurry. We need to get back to Jamie and the men,' Duncan said. 'Aaaa! Whit the....!!' From out of nowhere a man leapt onto his back. Another man lashed out at Donald, who only just managed to block the blow. Bending forward, Duncan threw the man on his back over his shoulders. The man hit the ground with a hard thump and lay motionless. Donald, although taken by surprise was slowly getting the better of Tom Comyn who, beaten, turned and ran.

* * * * * *

That evening as Jamie and his men were cooking the last of the deer that had been caught the previous day by one of the hunting parties. The door burst open and Duncan and Donald fell into the barn.

‘Where have you been? What happened?’ Jamie asked relieved.

‘We got Jock safely to the border. On the way back we came across a group of English soldiers out hunting,’ Donald stopped for breath. ‘If they’re the best archers in the world I’d hate to see the worst.’ They both laughed. 'They missed the deer by about ten foot.’

‘An’ nearly hit Donald,’ Duncan butted in. ‘Then once they had passed we were jumped by Tom Comyn an’ his cousin. He sneaked up behind us and jumped Donald, his cousin jumped me. If I hadnae been quick to throw him over my shoulders, I didnae know whit would hae happened. ’

‘If you had been on your guard they would ne’er hae sneaked up behind us,’ his brother reprimanded him.

‘If I‘d been on guard, whit aboot you? You were there too. Why did you no’ hear them sneak up on us?’ Duncan retaliated.

‘Enough. Where are Tom and his cousin now?’ Jamie asked.

‘It was a tough fight, his cousin is dead and Tom ran off. Tom'll be hurting after being beaten twice. He could be dangerous; nobody knows what he’ll do, Jamie,’ Duncan warned.

Jamie nodded in agreement. ‘He is already in the pay of the English. We will need to be extra vigilant. Now eat, you have a few hours to rest before we leave.’

‘Jamie! Jamie!’ the man throwing open the door to the barn paused to catch his breath. ‘Jamie!’

‘What is it man? Are you looking to alert the entire nation to our whereabouts?’

‘News,’ the man, who had been on watch for the past couple of hours, continued between breaths.

‘Your tenants, their homes have been destroyed and most of them are dead.’

‘How do you know, man?’ Jamie’s voice was unusually quiet.

‘We found a man dying in the woods he had been looking for you but had been attacked by some brigand or another. He is dead now, but he told us, he held on through the pain and blood loss long enough to tell us. He made us promise with his dying breath that we would tell you. I ran all the way here immediately. Patrick is burying the man in the woods.’

‘Jamie, are you alricht?’ Duncan asked as Jamie turned pale.

‘Jamie.' Without thinking, Mary ran up and flung her arms around his waist. ‘I’m sorry about your friends,' she whispered.

Jamie, patted her head gently. ‘Thank you, Mary.' Fighting back the tears and swallowing his emotion he addressed the men, ‘Tomorrow we get revenge.’

Chapter 5

'Jamie, can Donald and I hae a word?' Duncan asked after he and Donald had eaten.

'Aye, what is it?' Jamie asked, as the three of them moved into the shadows away from the fire, away from the other men.

'Mary,' after whispering with the twins for a few minutes, Jamie beckoned her, 'the twins think they may have spoken to your brother earlier. They met a boy a couple of years older than you. He had been captured by an English knight after his village had been attacked and burned,' Jamie said, not wanting to go into details about Malcolm trying to kill Sir Giles.

'Where?' Mary tried to hold back her excitement at the thought of Malcolm being alive.

'He was with a group of English noblemen who were out hunting. He couldn't leave with Duncan and Donald as it was too dangerous. He's in the castle with them. Where are you going?' Jamie asked as Mary headed towards the door.

Malcolm was a prisoner but at least that meant he was alive. She smiled. She wouldn't let him be a prisoner for long, she would go and rescue him, bring him back to join Jamie and his men. She had an axe. She might be a young girl but she would find a way of getting into the castle. 'I'm going to the castle to rescue my brother. I'll break down the drawbridge if I have to.'

Jamie laughed, 'Lass, you will not get close to the castle. You will be spotted miles off.'

'I'll crawl along the ground,' she said defiantly, upset and angry at being laughed at.

'Once you have broken through the portcullis you will encounter the garrison. How are you going to deal with them?'

‘I’ll…I’ll…I’ll...’ She couldn’t think of how to deal with an entire garrison of soldiers.

‘You can’t just attack the castle, it is too heavily defended. Surprise is the best means of taking it. I need time to think about the best approach. Now wait.’

She hesitated before sitting down. Malcolm was alive. She wasn’t alone in the world. She wanted to rescue him but she needed Jamie and his men to help her.

If Jamie could get revenge for the death of his tenants then she could get revenge for the death of her family and rescue Malcolm at the same time; Mary promised herself, the next morning as they set out to get revenge for the death of Jamie’s friends and tenants.

They hadn’t been riding for long when a man approached from the opposite direction. He rode straight up to Jamie. ‘I’ve met with our contact. Sir Giles is waiting in ambush, round the bend of the next hill,' the man, one of Jamie’s spies, informed him.

Jamie called to his men, ‘There are English soldiers waiting in ambush for us. There is every chance they outnumber us. What do you want to do? Take the long way round avoiding the ambush? Or attack?’

‘What about the death of your tenants?’ Duncan asked. ‘Are we going to leave them unavenged?’

‘No, if the soldiers waiting in ambush are from the castle, then they are likely to be the same ones who killed my tenants. We get our revenge here and now. What do you say, men?’

They all cheered.

‘Duncan, Donald, ride with me.’ Jamie signalled to the twins. The three of them, with Jamie in the middle, rode at the head of the group talking quietly together.

They continued on steadily until Jamie called a halt as they were riding along a broad, uneven path, hemmed in by hills on both sides. One hill was steep and craggy the other sloped gently up. A stream twisted and wove its way down its slope, it moved so slowly that Mary got the impression it wanted to stop and bask in the hot summer sun.

'This'll do.' Jamie looked from one twin to the other, who nodded; then calling out a dozen men to follow them, clambered up the slope. The others watched and waited below until their companions were more than halfway up.

'Men, draw you arms!' Jamie yelled, charging forward.

It all happened so fast. They turned a bend and clashed into the waiting men. Horses and men merged into one mass. Screams and shouts echoed like thunder, weapons sliced through the air. Then a dark shadow rushed down the slope to become one with the writhing, roaring beast. Bodies flew through the air or fell flailing to the ground. The occasional, contorted, grimacing face would appear for a second before disappearing back into the belly of the beast.

Mary sat safely, mounted behind Belle who had bypassed the ambush and was waiting close enough to join in the fighting if needed but far enough away to keep her safe. She turned her face away. This was nothing like she had imagined. Nothing like the ambushes they had in the village, where the girls would arm themselves with sticks and ambush the boys or the boys ambush the girls. The most they came away with were cuts and bruises. This time it was different, this time it was real. She wondered if she would ever be able to play that game again; without seeing and hearing the yelling, the fear, the injuries and the screams.

Finally, the noise of battle stopped and a strange stillness and silence hung in the air; then a horn blast broke the silence and figures broke off from the black mass, then horses were thundering towards them, but Belle wasn't moving, she was just waiting to be attacked. Just as Mary was going to yell at Belle to get out of the way she recognised Jamie and his men. As Belle swung her horse around beside Donald's she noticed a lone figure, standing on the site of the ambush. She could feel eyes staring at her, Malcolm is that you? She wondered as the figure shrunk into the distance.

After making sure none of the English soldiers were pursuing them, they pulled up to rest, patch up their wounds and let their horses drink.

'Ahem! Ahem!'

At the sound of the cough, Jamie spun round cursing drawing his sword; alerted by his cursing, the others were scrambling for their weapons.

'Finally, we found you,' one of the two tired, rough unkempt men who had suddenly appeared in their midst said raising his arms.

'Keith, Fraser, it is good to see you.' Jamie stepped forward, sheathing his sword as he greeted the two men cheerfully.

'It is good to see you too, Jamie.'

'What are you doing here?'

'Searching for you. We've been on your trail three days. We have come from King Robert with a message for you,' Keith explained.

'How goes it with the king? What news?'

'It goes well with King Robert and his army; if you can call a load of peasants, outlaws and highlanders an army,' the men laughed.

'Those men are Scotland's only hope,' Jamie cut in.

'Aye, I know that. They are starting to look more like an army and less like peasants and outlaws. There are not many highlanders; a few have come down from their hills and braes but not in large numbers. Promises of more have been made. Every day the King looks for the arrival of Angus Og from the Islands with his MacDonald clansmen; every day they do not appear.'

'Aye, we are beginning to think that they'll not come.' Fraser joined in the conversation.

Despondently Keith continued, 'Without them Jamie, who knows, you can say what you like about highlanders, barbarians most of them.' He winked cheekily at Duncan and Donald, 'But in a fight you want them on your side.'

'They will come,' Jamie said confidently.

'Why, Jamie, you're as optimistic as Bruce. He too has faith that the highlanders will come. That it is possible for the greatest army in Christendom to be beaten.'

'We have to have faith. Otherwise we would give up the fight.'

'We can't stay long,' Keith continued, nodding, 'the English army is finally on the move – or so we hear. Some of our men were involved in a small skirmish. Before one of the men died, he laughingly claimed that they were a forward party of the English army checking out the lie of the land and reporting back any news of the Scots army to King Edward. He laughed, ranting about how the Scots would soon all be dead.'

'Whoever they were they won't be laughing anymore, we saw to that,' Fraser said smiling.

'Fraser here led the Scots in that fight, something of which he is proud. All I hear from him is how he took this one down. How he avoided this blow and that blow. How at one point it was him against four.' Keith said teasingly.

'Well done, Fraser,' Jamie congratulated him, 'your first fight as a captain. But please what is your message?'

'King Robert wants you to cross the border and harass the English Army. That you delay their advance as much as you can; by whatever means possible. Whatever you do you have to make it harder for them to advance into Scotland. They will come no matter what, but you can buy the king and Scotland some more time.'

Jamie nodded, 'Is that all?'

'No, on your way back you have to meet up with Randolph – who is besieging the castle – and help him take it. Time is running out and the king can not afford to have you and Randolph away too long so be quick.'

'It will be done.'

'If any man can buy Bruce and Scotland a couple of days you can. We have to go now, Jamie, return to the army and help prepare it to face the battle ahead.' With that the two men mounted. 'Oh, Jamie I nearly forgot, Ian McRhuari will be joining you with some men.' They disappeared as quickly as they had arrived.

'Ian McRhuari,' Jamie said quietly. Ian McRhuari had recently come over to the side of the Scots. Although stubborn, he was a good fighter and commander. Most of his men were archers and would be useful. 'I'll be glad of all the help I can get.'

'Men, we ride into England in the morning.' Jamie informed them. 'The best place to attack the enemy is in a valley some distance over the border. There we can use the land to our advantage.'

'Whit aboot the pass? Can we no' attack them there?' Donald asked.

Jamie shook his head. 'Too risky. We would need to attack at exactly the right moment. If the enemy got too far in they could escape through the pass if they did not get in far enough they could turn heel. No, the valley is the best option.'

They spent the rest of the day tending to their wounds, washing in the river and making plans for the upcoming fight.

That night Mary wrapped in a cloak, lay under a bush; listening to the sound of Belle, who lay near her snoring. The sound of a twig snapping and hurried footsteps distracted her from her thoughts. Turning towards the sounds she was in time to witness Hugh and Walter slip away into the darkness.

'Where are you going?' she asked quietly. Not that she really cared where they were going as long as they didn't come back. She didn't like Hugh and Walter, neither did she trust them. More than once she had caught one or the other staring at her with a look that sent a chill through her.

Maybe she should follow them and see where they were going? Or waken Jamie and tell him. As she was making up her mind, another movement forced her to lie still, Jamie stealthily following Hugh and Walter. Was he going to meet them secretly away from the rest of the men she wondered? For the first time she had her doubts about whether or not to trust Jamie. I'll do it! I'll go and find out if Jamie is good or bad.

'Go back to sleep.' Mary had only taken a few paces when Belle, her eyes still closed, spoke.

'How?...You were sleeping?'

'This is war. It's not safe to sleep too soundly.'

'But, Jamie?'

'Mary, go back to sleep.' Belle opened her eyes. 'Leave Jamie to find out what Hugh and Walter are up to.'

Mary nodded and lay down again. 'I'll just lie here and wait until Belle is really asleep then I'll find out if

I can trust Jamie or not.' she thought, glancing over at Belle, who lay snoring, seemingly sound asleep. But was she? She had thought Belle had been asleep a few minutes ago but she hadn't been. She would sit here and wait until she was sure; then she would follow Jamie.

The sun had hardly risen when Jamie wakened them.

'We need to leave in an hour,' he informed them. 'Belle, you and Donald take the watch. Duncan, take a couple of men and see if you can find us something to eat. Be quick.'

As soon as Belle and the twins had left to carry out their respective tasks and Jamie's attention was on his horse, Hugh, returned from his night's adventure, sidled up to her.

He lowered his voice, 'Your family was killed cos' of Jamie.'

'What?' She spun round to face him. 'You lie.'

Hugh shook his head slowly. 'Your family was killed cos' of Jamie.' he repeated clearly.

Was he telling the truth? Was Jamie, a man she trusted, with whom she felt safe, responsible for the attack on her village and for Malcolm being a prisoner?

'I don't believe you.' She hoped her voice hid her uncertainty. 'I need to...,' she never told Hugh what she needed to do. Instead she walked off, her head spinning. Was Jamie responsible for the attack on her village? And if he was why was he looking after her, why was she not dead too? It wasn't like he didn't have the opportunity. No, Hugh must be wrong; it was some joke on his part. She walked on, unable to shake the feeling that she had trusted the man responsible for Malcolm being a prisoner and the death of her parents. She was worried about Malcolm. Had he abandoned her and gone over to the English? She had seen him as he watched them ride off after the ambush; he could easily have followed them but hadn't done so.

Hugh laughed quietly to himself, 'You're doing exactly as I want, little girl,' before winking at Walter who slinked off to follow her.

Her mind wandering, her thoughts in turmoil, she walked on; until the ground shook. Stealing a glance over her shoulder; she saw the demon chasing her. This demon was bigger than any of the others. She screamed, but her scream was drowned out by the roar of nearby flames. Blindly, disorientated by the thick smoke she ran first in one direction then another. She was unable to see clearly through the smoke, through her stinging eyes that were now filling with water. Now the demon was in front of her she turned to run in the opposite direction but the demon was still in front of her. She turned again; still the demon was in front of her. Side stepping past it her foot searched desperately for firm ground; there was none. She tumbled forward, rolling out of the smoke, gaining speed as she rolled over stones, yelling as her head hit the roots of a bush, until she splashed to a halt in a muddy stream.

A large hand stretched down and picked her up.

'Are you hurt?' the voice attached to the hand asked.

Slowly, lifting her head up to answer she opened her eyes, there was no smoke, no demon; only a kindly face. She shook her head in answer. As she looked up at the man, she caught sight of Hugh and Walter standing on the edge of the slope looking down on her.

The man smiled. 'Good. Now will you join us here until you get your breath back?' The man, holding out a large hand, helped her to her feet and led her behind a rock where a fire burned. Another man sat by the fire, stirring the contents of a pot. Two horses, more magnificent than any she had seen before, were tethered nearby.

Still stunned from her fall, she obediently took a seat by the fire. One of the men handed her a bowl of food. She ate. He handed her a drink. She drank, not once having taken her eyes off the men.

'Are you going to kill me?' she spurted out.

'Why? Because we are English and you are Scottish?' the man with the big hands asked.

She reddened.

'Would we have fed you if we were going to kill you?' the man who had been stirring the pot asked. 'We are messengers from King Edward with a message for the Lord of the castle nearby. We have no desire to kill you or any Scots.'

'I'm Mary,' she introduced herself, relieved that she wasn't going to be killed.

'Hello Mary, I am….' He never got a chance to finish. The point of a dagger appeared over the top of the rock. Another one appeared round the side. A figure appeared in front of them dagger in hand. Mary jumped then smiled relieved.

'Found you. The twins were worried,' Belle smiled.

'Aye, we were worried,' the twins said together as they came round the rock.

'Who are you?' Belle, moving her hand to the axe hanging by her side, demanded of the men.

Out of the corner of her eye, Mary saw Duncan and Donald reach for their swords.

'We are messengers from King Edward with a message for the lord of the nearby castle. We come in peace.'

'Deliver your message. Go in peace but go now,' Donald said sharply, putting his hand on Mary's shoulder and leading her away.

'Thank you for feeding me.' She waved to the messengers as she left with Belle and the twins.

'How did you find me?' she asked Donald as he led her away.

'We were ready to leave when Jamie noticed you were gone.' He added under his breath, 'and Hugh and Walter were missing tae, he sent us tae find you.'

The rest of the walk continued in silence. When they reached the place where they had been resting Jamie was waiting.

'Mary, where have you been?' he demanded angrily.

'I went for a walk,' she wanted to shout, 'I know, I know that my family are dead because of you.' Yet Jamie had always been kind to her, had never shown any sign of wanting to hurt her. Maybe Hugh had been lying after all, lying to get her on her own, but why? She wouldn't say anything now, she would wait.

'Never wander off on your own. It is too dangerous,' Jamie continued, berating her. 'I thought you would have learned that at Old Jock's. Can I trust you? If not I will send you to join King Robert.'

Tears welled up in her eyes. 'I'm sorry. Please let me stay with you. I won't wander off again. I want to stay with you. I am not afraid.' Her voice was quiet, pleading. She wanted to stay with Jamie despite what Hugh had said. She wanted to stay with Duncan, Donald and Belle to return their kindness to her. 'I have my dagger. I want to fight for Scotland.'

'If you wander off again I will leave you behind to suffer your fate.' Although Jamie was trying to sound stern the anger had gone from his voice. 'You have delayed our departure long enough and put my men in danger by having to search for you.' Jamie blew his horn. 'We must go now.'

The horn blast brought the missing men back in groups of threes and fours. There was no sign of Hugh and Walter.

'What're we going to do about Hugh and Walter, Jamie?' Belle stood in front of him, hands on her hips.

'What do you mean?'

'I don't trust them. They know our plans, where we are heading. They could bring the enemy to us.'

'We have to take the risk.'

'There is another way. Hunt them down. We know what deaths they have caused. Who knows what deaths they might cause in the future? Hunt them down. Why should they live?'

Jamie, spoke softly. 'Belle, I too believe that they caused the death of your brothers and understand you wanting revenge. I would happily go with you to hunt them down and let you deal with them as you may. Now, is not the time. There is no time. We must fight; win this battle before we can fight our own.'

Belle, stood sometime not moving, the hard look in her eyes softened by a hint of sadness. Then she relaxed, a smile crossed her face and she nodded, 'Aye, Jamie, Scotland first then the traitors. Let's go.'

Jamie looked relieved. 'Come, we must leave now. Stay with Belle and the twins. They will protect you,' he whispered to Mary as Belle helped her on to her horse.

* * * * * *

'Are you in league with James Douglas!!?' Sir Giles demanded.

Malcolm didn't hear him, things had gone wrong. His good deed had backfired and the ambush had been his fault; men were dead or injured because of him. If he hadn't misdirected the hunting party so the two men in the woods could escape, Sir Giles would never have learned that the Scots were close by.

He had been congratulating himself on his quick thinking, when Sir Giles had pulled up abruptly and addressed a man – he called Tom – who was blocking the way. It was at that point that his plan had started to fall apart and his pride abate.

Tom had looked at and spoken to Sir Giles with flattery and admiration and everybody else with contempt – a contempt that was returned. Initially, he had looked at Malcolm with a look of contempt which had, slowly, changed into a knowing smile. A smile that made Malcolm wish he could shoot an arrow straight through one of Tom's eyes. That feeling grew as the conversation between Sir Giles and Tom continued.

'Who were the men?' Malcolm's ears pricked up at Sir Giles' question. Tom had been mumbling something about being attacked by two men in the forest; their description matched the men he had been talking to.

'Two of James Douglas' men, Duncan and Donald Campbell.'

So, that's who they were. Why had they been in the woods and hiding? Had they been waiting to attack Tom? But where had Tom been hiding? He hadn't seen anyone else in the woods. Had Tom spotted him talking to the men and would he tell Sir Giles? His hand moved to his bow.

'You're a fool if you thought you could beat them in a fight.' Sir Giles sneered.

Tom looked peevish. 'I thought it would be easy as they weren't paying attention.'

'You are a bigger fool than I thought. They are two of the best fighters I have ever seen – even if they were in chains you wouldn't stand a chance against them!'

For a split second Tom looked like he was going to choke with anger. Then he had taken his opportunity.

'That young lad was talking to them,' he said pointing at Malcolm.

Malcolm had shaken his head as all eyes turned towards him.

'Is that true?' Sir Giles asked.

He had stared hard at Sir Giles. He was not going to tell that man anything. He was not going to be intimidated by him. If only he hadn't let Duncan and Donald talk him out of shooting the arrow he would get his revenge. Somehow.

'Well, boy!!'

'They spoke to me.'

'Do you know them?'

'No.'

'He knew them alright!' Tom said with relish. If he couldn't get the girl he would cause trouble for the boy. The boy who helped James Douglas, the man he hated more than anyone except Robert Bruce.

'Did you know them?' Sir Giles had looked from Tom to Malcolm, then back again.

Slowly, he had shaken his head so everybody there could see it. 'No, I only learned their names when this man said them earlier. I've never seen the men before.'

Sir Giles had stared at him for a long time as if trying to decide whether to believe him or not. He must have decided to believe him or more than likely he had decided that hunting was more important as he changed the subject.

'Do you know where James Douglas is camped?' Sir Giles leant forward on his horse as he spoke. Tom shook his head.

'But, my friend Hugh' - at the mention of Hugh, a strange look passed over Sir Alexander's face - 'told me they'll be riding south tomorrow or the following day.'

Tom hadn't finished speaking when Sir Giles rode off, deliberately knocking him over as he passed.

'Good riddance.' Malcolm had to resist the temptation to spit on Tom who lay sprawled on the ground. The depth of his feeling against Tom shocked him, scared him almost. He had only met the man a few minutes previously, but hated him with a passion. I'm glad I'll not see that man again, he had thought as he caught up with Sir Giles.

How wrong he had been about that. They had returned to the castle a few hours later after an unsuccessful hunt. Sir Giles had blamed him for the failure. He had led them down the left fork away from the good hunting ground. Lead them on a chase against an imaginary stag. Sir Giles' temper hadn't improved when he spotted Tom waiting to greet him.

Then there had been the ambush. Sir Giles had appeared the following morning, with a suit of chainmail and orders to meet in the courtyard within the hour. They had all been there, the nobles and their squires from the previous day's hunting party and the foot soldiers. All except Sir Alexander who appeared, harassed and looking furtive from outside the castle half an hour later.

'Where have you been?' Sir Giles whose temper had increased with every minute spent waiting, challenged.

'My horse is lame so the stable boy lent me this one. I wanted to see how she rides.' Sir Alexander patted the horse's neck looking and sounding more relaxed.

On the way out of the castle Malcolm passed Sir Alexander and heard him murmur to himself, 'You're a fool, Alexander, a fool, do you hear! You nearly destroyed everything.' His horse had stumbled on uneven ground but hadn't shown any sign of injury. This morning, one of its front legs was badly swollen. The stable hand reckoned it would clear in a few days and had given him the Chestnut to ride – it rode well and would do. The concern over his horse had caused him to be careless of time, he sighed relieved that Sir Giles had believed his lie and that the consequences of his lateness hadn't been worse.

What had he nearly destroyed and how? Malcolm wanted to ask as they followed Sir Giles to the point he had chosen for the ambush

They hadn't long reached the ambush site when the Scots had arrived, charging around the curve of the hill yelling their war cry, 'A Douglas! A Douglas!'

The front rider had crashed into him head on; it had only been fear that had kept him from toppling from his horse. He had been battered and bashed by legs and arms, thumped by the rump of charging horses. He had been so scared and gripping the reins of his horse so hard that his knuckles had turned white.

A sword, momentarily, hung in the air above his head. The blade sharp and glistening, slowly, every second feeling like a minute, it had come closer and closer to him. I'm going to die here and now, he thought, die in sight of Mary. He had noticed, or at least thought he had noticed before he was overcome by fear, the horse breaking away from the charging group and riding into the distance and had recognised Mary. 'I've let you down,' he whispered barely moving his lips as the sword covered the last few centimetres, it came within millimetres of his shoulder before the man wielding it charged past and on to some else. He had breathed a sigh of relief which had turned into a scream when another sword came at him. He had wanted to reach for his sword, but his hands wouldn't leave the reins. The sword was inches from him. This sword wasn't going to miss; it had been aimed perfectly for his head. Then another sword appeared under the first one cutting its fall short.

'Not that one!' a voice said at his side. Then a hand grabbed the reins and tried to pull him free. What was happening? Who was trying to rescue him? He had wanted to help but couldn't. The hand let go as an axe, then a sword blade flashed past Malcolm's face. Men fell at his feet and the rider who had tried to rescue him had been pushed back by three or four men.

He had hated every long minute of the ambush, the blades passing close to his face, the danger, the yelling and groaning of the injured. All his life he had dreamt of one day being a soldier; no longer. Now he wanted to be an archer. He had frozen with fear. When it was all over he had thought about forcing his way through the crumbling ambush but couldn't even manage that.

One good thing had come from it, Mary was alive.

Now, he had Sir Giles to deal with. A Sir Giles who was not only angry but humiliated by all the defeats and set backs.

'Are you listening to me?!'

Sullenly, he inclined his head.

'Are you in league with James Douglas?' Sir Giles, roared covering Malcolm in spit as he did so.

That question again. How could he be? How could he possibly pass messages to the Scots, when the only times he had left the castle had been in the company of Sir Giles?

'Calm down, Giles.' Sir Alexander came to Malcolm's assistance.

‘Calm down! Calm down!? We were humiliated today. The Scots were prepared for us. They knew we were waiting. How unless someone had told them?’

‘And you think Malcolm informed them of the whereabouts of the ambush? Do you think he climbed over the castle wall, hunted down the Scots and then climbed back in?’ Sir Alexander’s voice was steady and clear.

It amazed Malcolm how alone amongst the nobles, Sir Alexander showed no fear of Sir Giles, in fact he seemed to take great pleasure in challenging him or making a fool of him.

‘Not exactly,’ Sir Giles, replied through gritted teeth.

‘How then? I’m curious to know how you think Malcolm, has been passing messages to James Douglas when the only time he has left the castle has been in your company? Ah, that’s it..,’ Sir Alexander clicked his fingers, ‘I have it. You are passing messages to James Douglas. It must be you and you are blaming Malcolm to divert suspicion. Good, very good, Sir Giles. I would bow to you in respect. But, I am afraid as a traitor to the King of England, you do not deserve respect.’

‘I, a traitor….,’ the word seemed to catch in Sir Giles’ throat and unable to respond he stormed off, stopping once. ‘Don’t think this is the end of it, boy. I’ll be watching you from now on.’

After Sir Giles’ departure Malcolm found himself left alone with Sir Alexander.

‘Thank you,’ he said quietly, still unable to believe what he had just witnessed.

‘No, thank you. I relish the opportunity to get back at that arrogant man.’

‘How? Why? I mean….’

'Why do I dare to say the things I do to Sir Giles, when anybody else's head would be on the block? Because, young Malcolm, I have the fortune or misfortune to be related to the King of England. My mother is his favourite aunt and Sir Giles can not touch me as by doing so he would suffer the wrath of King Edward and find his own head on the block.' Sir Alexander laughed. 'What is it? I can see from your face that you want to ask me something else? Don't be afraid of me, Malcolm, I won't hurt you and I'll protect you best I can.'

Something about Sir Alexander's tone reassured him. 'That man, Tom Comyn, who is he?'

'Tom Comyn? He believes that he should be King of Scots!' Malcolm looked shocked. 'Not him personally,' Sir Alexander went on, laughing, 'but his cousin. That is why he hates King Robert because he thinks he stole his family's throne. He hates anybody who supports King Robert. Now, Malcolm, I have to freshen up and get myself in the right frame of mind to face a meal with those men. So, I take my leave. Don't worry Sir Giles will calm down soon.'

When Sir Alexander had left, he wandered off to loose some arrows. Arrow after arrow hit the target.

'What are you doing?' Simon asked, running across the courtyard towards him.

'Shooting arrows.'

'Yes, but you are doing it angry. Never loose an arrow angry, it will make you careless.'

As Malcolm turned to respond to Simon, he caught a movement out of the side of his eye. Tom, sneaking and slinking in the background, watching his every move. His anger overwhelmed him. He raised his bow and shot an arrow straight at Tom which fortunately missed and recoiled of a nearby pillar.

'Are you trying to get in trouble?' Simon slapped the bow down to the side. 'Never do that again!'

'You can't be trusted with that!' Malcolm looked up as a hand wrenched the bow away from him.

'Give me my bow!' Malcolm, demanded, making a grab for it.

Sir Giles raised the bow above his head.

'Why do you have to destroy everything I hold dear?'

'You destroyed that yourself – when you helped James Douglas.' Sir Giles stormed off waving Malcolm's bow tauntingly above his head.

Angry, Malcolm ran. He ran, exhausted, the anger, the hate and confusion getting the better of him all the way to the top of the tower. He hated Sir Giles, he hated Tom, he hated James Douglas and this stupid war. Why did Jamie have to come to his father for help? Why!? If he hadn't asked for their help his village would never have been destroyed, his family would still be together. Why could King Robert not just let King Edward have the throne? It was a stupid throne anyway and a stupid war. He kicked the door shut, and then kicked it again wishing he was kicking Sir Giles, King Edward, even King Robert. It was all their fault. He shouted stamping his feet, pacing angrily up and down, cursing and swearing at everybody until exhausted, he slept.

'What's the matter?' John was standing over him when he woke.

'Why should there be something wrong?'

'Cause your face is all red and I heard you curse and swear last night.'

'You heard me?'

'I heard you but thought it best to leave you alone. Now out with it!'

'Sir Giles took my bow from me. Just as he took my home and my family.'

'That isn't fair.' John stood looking thoughtfully at him then held out his hand.

'Up, let's go get your bow.' He bent down and helped Malcolm to his feet.

'How?'

'Easy, if Sir Alexander will help.' John winked

Not quite sure where they were going, or how they were going to get his bow back he let John lead him down to the second level of the castle.

'Stay in there until I return.' John ordered pushing Malcolm into a dark alcove. 'I won't be long.'

John disappeared down the stairs.

Left on his own he tried to make sense of events. John was helping him because he liked adventure. But why would he think that Sir Alexander would help? John had told him that Sir Alexander would do anything to get one over on Sir Giles; Sir Alexander had even admitted that himself, but was that it? He remembered the look on Sir Alexander's face when Tom had mentioned Hugh; it was as if he had got the answer to a long unanswered question. Then there was the morning of the ambush, when he had claimed to be out riding to get use to a new horse. Was that the truth? Or was it Sir Alexander who had warned the Scots about the ambush? Was he in league with the Scots, as Sir Giles would say?

'Malcolm, Malcolm.' John's whisper brought him out of his reverie.

'I'm here.'

'Sssshhhh!!!! Sir Alexander is keeping watch and will let us know if Sir Giles returns. Hurry.'

They stole along the corridor, keeping in the shadows until they reached large double doors under which light flickered. He held his breath expecting Sir

Giles or one of the other nobles to appear at any minute as John, without hesitation pushed open the door. As his eyes adjusted to the low light they opened wider; he had never seen such luxury. The bed was bigger than his home had been. The curtains hanging from it were purple velvet. He gingerly ran his hand over the silk bedding. Tapestries, depicting hunting scenes and fine maidens, more beautiful than anything he had ever seen hung from the walls. A large fire burned in a fireplace that took up more than quarter of the wall.

'One day when I find my father's treasure I am going to have luxury like this,' John declared as he helped himself to a handful of coins that had been flung carelessly on to a chest.

Malcolm shook his head in mock shock at John's theft, he didn't really think John would find the treasure or that it even existed, but John seemed to believe it.

'Now, where's your bow?'

Malcolm reluctantly pulled his eyes from the riches and moved them around the room, surely in amongst all the finery his poor bow would be easy to spot. He looked all around, his bow was no where to be seen.

'It must be here somewhere,' he mumbled, 'but where?'

His eyes lighted on the fire. He wouldn't have, would he? Sir Giles wouldn't have burnt his bow, he couldn't be that bad! With images of his beautiful bow being burnt to a crisp and the noise of John scuffling around, he headed to the fire. He knelt down and leaned towards the fire, the heat turning his face instantly red.

'Found it,' John declared, in a loud whisper, holding the bow triumphantly.

Malcolm jumped up, grabbing the bow with one hand while he hugged John with the other. 'Where did you find it?'

'Under the bed.' John's smile stretched from ear to ear. 'We'd better hurry. Sir Alexander won't be able to delay Sir Giles too long if he decides to return to his room.'

John closed the door quietly behind them and they headed for the top of the stairs where Sir Alexander was leaning against the wall waiting.

'Ahh! I see you got your bow back. Good, good. I'm glad. But keep it out of Sir Giles' way. If he doesn't see you with it he will forget it existed and you and it will be safe.'

Chapter 6

Malcolm lay curled up in his alcove, listening to the scratching of a rat running along the floor, watching the last dying embers of the fire, shivering in the cold breeze that blew under the door. He pulled his bow closer to him; archery was the only thing he cared about since his family had been destroyed and nobody was going to take it from him. Since he and John had retrieved the bow from Sir Giles, he had expected that man to appear at any moment, grab the bow, break it and throw him into the dungeons. Then there was Tom; who was everywhere he was, making him feel uncomfortable, watching and spying on him he sensed that if he even touched a bow Sir Giles would be informed immediately.

He stood up, stretching: he would go to the battlements. They were the only place he could be free. At first, even although he had been accompanied by Simon, the soldiers had been suspicious of him but they eventually got use to his presence and they now let him sit with them in the guardroom or let him be on the battlements as long as he didn't get in their way. None of the soldiers liked Tom. The first time Tom had followed him on to the battlements the soldiers had taunted him and made a fool of him. Another time they had beaten him up – he felt guilty about that now, he knew he should have intervened but he liked seeing that man suffer.

From the battlements he could look down on those who normally looked down on him. He watched Tom, sneaking and lurking about, fawning over Sir Giles and the other nobles. He had watched laughing as Sir Giles stood in the courtyard, shouting for his squire; when Malcolm hadn't appeared he had sent a servant to look for him. When the servant returned alone, Sir

Giles had ridden off, spurring and whipping the horse in anger. Sir Giles wasn't the only one who went riding alone, some mornings Sir Alexander rode out, alone. He would leave as the sun rose and be back before the other nobles were up and about. Malcolm, had spent many a morning watching him gallop over the horizon trying to figure out what he was doing.

'Good morning!'

'How you are, son?'

The soldiers, who were standing or sitting listlessly in the heat, greeted him as soon as he stepped on to the battlements.

'Good morning!' he greeted them in turn.

He took up his usual position, at the front just to the left of the entrance; from where he got the best view without disturbing the guards. He would stand for hours, looking into the distance. Not that there was anything to see, apart from Sir Alexander.

This time things were different, there was movement on the horizon. Slight, hazy and blurred but movement none the less. Figures, making their way to the castle. Slowly they came into view, men on horseback, men marching, pack horses, carts with supplies; an army. He stood staring at the approaching army, his mind full of conflicting thoughts. Were they coming to join the garrison or a Scottish army preparing to attack? If they were Scots it could be his chance to escape. He watched the army as they came closer. He had decided that it was a Scottish army as he wanted to believe it was. His eyes, darted from left to right in a hope of spotting Mary, although he knew it was a small hope.

* * * * *

'Belle, are you a' richt to keep Mary wi' you? Or do you want me to tak' her for a spell?' Donald asked as they set off again after resting their horses.

‘I’m fine keeping her, Donald.’

‘Just as well, because riding wi’ Donald she would be tossed an’ bumped aboot,’ Duncan interjected.

‘Hey, I‘m a better rider than you,’ Donald argued.

‘Nay, I’m a far better rider,’ Duncan retaliated.

‘If you two weren’t so reliable in a fight I would leave you behind, with all you’re arguing.’ Jamie shouted over his shoulder as he led the rest of the men towards the border. Looking back Mary laughed as the twins quickly rushed to catch up.

‘I like the twins,’ she whispered, grasping tighter to Belle. She did not want to leave Belle’s side in case Hugh and Walter turned up again. She felt that Belle and the twins would protect her no matter what.

‘Don’t hold so tight, Mary.’ Belle breathed in relief as Mary reluctantly loosened her grip. ‘I like them too. Sometimes you would think they hated each other the way they go on. But if you dare wrong one of them; all their differences are forgotten and you have to deal with both of them.’

They rode on long and hard, all through the night and most of the following day.

‘We will rest here awhile,’ Jamie said to his men when they arrived at a clearing. ‘Donald, take six men with you and keep watch.’

Donald nodded and signalled to the men nearest him to follow.

‘Why are we stopping ‘ere? If you want to get tae the valley afore the English should we no’ be further south?’ Duncan asked.

‘Aye, but you are exhausted as are the horses.’ Jamie looked around at his men as they lit a fire, found bushes and trees to sleep under for warmth and protection. Only those on guard duty wouldn’t be sleeping.

‘We ‘ave pushed on exhausted before.’

'It ain't just the men it's the horses and Mary.'

'I dinnae like it. It doesnae feel richt. I don't trust…,' Duncan said lowering his voice.

'Who don't you trust?'

'Donald!'

'Your brother?'

'No! Donald!' Duncan pushed Jamie out the way as he ran towards his brother who had appeared amongst them bloody and bruised.

'Whit happened?'

'Hugh and Walter, with some others jumped me. Willie is dead. I fought my way out.'

'I'll see tae them,' Duncan stormed off to find Hugh.

'No, Duncan. Wait.' Belle blocked his path.

'Oot my way.'

'No. You can't.' Belle stood firm.

'Why no? They killed your brothers and you want revenge. Why can't I?'

'You can, but not like this. If it was only Hugh and Walter, yes. I would even come with you. But they are not alone; Donald only just managed against five or six and he had Willie to help. How are you going to manage against ten times that? Cause, there will be. Why only attack Donald? When there are others on guard. Think, Duncan.'

'She's right, Duncan, I heard them. There are men nearby by preparing to attack.' Donald fell to his knees, blood pouring from a wound.

'Form up,' Jamie ordered. 'You don't have to.' Jamie looked with concern at Donald who had risen unsteadily to his feet.

'Aye, I dae. I can breathe, so I can fight,' Donald said defiantly as, trying not to stagger, he took his place beside Duncan.

Mary grabbed her axe and formed up with them.

'No, Mary, you go and hide stay out the way.' Jamie pointed to a nearby bush.

'Why can't I stay with you?' She wanted to be close to the men so the demons wouldn't get her.

'You need strength, determination and great skill to fight in a schiltron.' Mary watched as the men stood in a group, the front row armed with swords pointing up and leaning against their feet, the rows behind them had their weapons pointing out over the shoulders of the men in front, all were tightly compacted. 'You need to be able to move, to turn and fight in any direction without breaking ranks. That takes practise. You will be safer hiding.'

As she lay under the bush she slipped her axe under her body; if the demons attacked this time she would fight back, she promised herself, although she wasn't sure she would keep the promise. She curled up making herself small, pushing herself as far into the ground as possible, so the demons wouldn't see her.

She had hardly hidden herself when the sound of running feet and shouts reached them. She looked through a space between two branches. As Jamie and his men looking at each other in silent agreement prepared themselves to face the enemy, men and horses came running through the trees charging from all sides. The attack was vicious.

She covered her ears and shut her eyes. If her friends died what would become of her? Where would she go? She could make her way back to the village to see if anyone had survived, but she had only left the village a couple of times and didn't know where she was. Her only hope was that at least one of Jamie's men would survive and keep her with him or that some other kindly soul would take pity on her. More than likely she would die out here alone.

The screams, shouts and clashing of metal continued. Finally, curiosity overcame her fear and she opened her eyes and immediately wished she hadn't.

Not only were Jamie's tired and exhausted men collapsing under the onslaught. But Hugh was standing in front of her.

'Got you this time. Altho' you are no guid to me now with Jamie defeated.' He bent down and lifted her to her feet.

Thwang! Thwack!

Hugh stepped back, letting go of Mary, a second before an arrow whizzed over the spot where he had been standing. As soon as she was free of his grip she moved further into hiding. The arrow was followed by horses crashing out of the trees, their riders letting off arrow after arrow. Those riders not armed with bows were cutting and slicing with swords and axes. Hugh started to run but was halted by an arrow piercing his body. At the arrival of the newcomers, Jamie's men recovered enough to put up a last fight, before falling exhausted to the ground. It all seemed to be over in a flash.

'Ian, I am glad to see you.' Jamie greeted the leader of the new arrivals. 'You have perfect timing.'

'What happened here?'

'Traitors and betrayal.'

Ian shook his head. 'My men will take over guard duty. You get yours rested.'

Jamie looked uncertain.

'You can trust me, Jamie. I am on the side of Bruce and Scotland.'

Jamie nodded, and helped his men see to the dead and injured. Mary looked for Walter, hoping that he had not run off with the rest. She found him amongst the dead, Hugh lying by his side. Raising her foot she kicked Hugh vengefully; he wouldn't feel it but it made her feel better. Turning to Walter she stepped on his arm. He groaned. She jumped back in fright. As she walked over to join the others standing over Donald, who lay bleeding on the ground, she didn't notice Ian walk up to Walter and finish him off.

'Donald!' Duncan shouted as he fell to his knees and took his brother in his arms.

'Donald, dinnae die.'

'Duncan,' Donald got out as his eyes closed.

Her heart breaking, Mary turned back towards the bodies of Hugh and Walter. 'If you have killed Donald, I hope you never rest in peace,' she cursed the dead men. This was all their fault. She had never hated as much as she hated Hugh and Walter and had never feared as much as she feared the demons. 'This is all your fault!' Not caring if they sat up and spoke and needing to vent her hatred she stamped hard on both the bodies. 'Take that!'

Jamie crouched down beside Duncan and placed his hand on Donald's forehead.

'He is still alive. He will survive.' He tried to reassure Duncan but his voice was filled with fear and worry. 'Ian, can you spare some men to take the injured to Thomas' camp? He is laying siege to the castle nearby.' Ian nodded.

'I'm goin' tae.' Duncan tried to hold back the tears.

'No, Duncan I need you with me.' Jamie laid his arm on Duncan's who stared back at him, before nodding quietly. 'You will see you brother again.'

Early the next morning, having left men behind to bury the dead, white faced and heavy eyed they crossed the border into England. They had been riding for a couple of hours when a mounted man approached them; he ignored Jamie and headed straight for Ian MacRhuari. The two men spoke in urgent tones then the newcomer rode off in the direction he had come.

'Jamie,' Ian made his way to Jamie's side, 'before I joined you I sent some of my fastest riders on ahead to keep me updated with the movements of the English army. I have just received a message that the English army are coming on at such a rate that they will be past the valley in an hour or two. We will never make it in time.'

'An hour or two! Curse Hugh and Walter! Their treachery has delayed us. The pass… it will have to be the pass. We must hurry or they will be in Scotland before we can stop them,' Jamie shouted urging his men on.

Galloping at full speed they reached the pass within the hour. Quietly and steadily, almost holding their breath, they made their way up the slope. The horses accustomed as they were to the rough Scottish countryside found it hard going, slipping and sliding with almost every step. There were a couple of near misses when their hooves slipped on loose rocks. Finally, all the men reached the top safely.

As she dismounted from Duncan's horse, Mary looked over the edge of the steep slope, covered in rocks and stones it fell at a steep angle down towards a narrow path, both sides of which were lined with trees.

'How do you plan to take the enemy unaware here?' Ian McRhuari asked Jamie.

'My plan is to use the land and the trees to our advantage. We will split up. Attack from different points, make as much noise as possible and hopefully the enemy will think they are under attack from a far larger force.'

'That easy is it? Do you think the English army is just going to stand here and let you attack them?' Ian sounded doubtful.

'No I don't, but that is where my young friend Mary can help and your archers come in.'

'How can I help?' Mary asked desperate to be of use.

'See that boulder about three quarters of the way down the slope?'

'Yes,' she said quietly, thinking that Jamie was going to tell her to hide and stay out the way again.

'I want you to collect as many stones and rocks as possible, then hide behind that rock. At my signal throw them down amongst the soldiers, with Ian's archers attacking at the same time. That should cause enough confusion to enable the rest of us to attack unawares. Can you do that?'

'Yes.'

'Good. Go now. We only have a couple of hours until the enemy will be on us.'

Gingerly, she headed down the slope, moving more confidently once she had found her footing, collecting stones as she went and throwing them down towards the rock to be gathered up later. She worked quietly away by herself until a large pile of stones lay beside her, ready to be put into action.

While she worked Jamie and Ian gathered their men together; they must have been given out orders as the men split into groups and hid themselves at different points amongst the trees on both sides of the pass; still others started gathering stones; the archers positioned themselves at various points along the hillside.

With all the preparations made and the men in place. Jamie came to speak to her. 'That is a large number of rocks and stones you have collected. Well done. Are you sure you want to do this?'

'I want to help. I'm not afraid.' She said the last part more to convince herself than Jamie.

'Good I'm glad. Now stay down, the enemy will be here soon.' He turned to walk away.

'Please, Jamie,' Mary stopped him in his tracks.

'What is it, lass?'

'You said that I was to start throwing the stones when I heard your signal.'

'That's correct.'

'What is your signal?'

Jamie laughed, 'I was forgetting that this is your first time fighting with me. I will sound this horn twice.' He raised the horn that hung by his side. She nodded her understanding and Jamie headed down the slope and disappeared amongst the trees.

She was by herself. Her companions spread out. They were all relying on her, the other stone throwers and the archers to cause enough confusion to distract the English army so that they would not be able to put up a good fight.

'You can't let your friends down, Mary. Throw the stones as hard as you can,' she mumbled to herself as she picked the first stone up so she would be ready as soon as she heard the signal. 'You are doing this for Malcolm, for your parents, for Scotland.'

A few minutes later she caught sight of the sun glinting on metal as the enemy approached. They came on at a quick rate, coming ever closer until half of them were in the pass.

The sound of the horn being blown twice reached her ears. One after another she hurled and rolled the stones down the slope. The first few missed their target but she soon corrected her aim so as the stones were falling into the middle of the enemy alongside the arrows.

Trapped in the pass, the English were in confusion, looking all around trying to see who was flinging the stones and firing the arrows, while trying to use their shields and in some cases their arms as protection. Some of the stones hit the horses who reared and threw their riders, who took down two or three of their companions as they fell. Others hit men who yelled and shouted. Every minute she expected to see soldiers head up the slope to hunt her down. No one appeared so she continued to throw the stones even when her arms hurt.

The horn blew again but carried away Mary, kept on throwing stones until the archers waving frantically at her, caught her attention and signalled to her to stop. As her last stone landed and the noise it made bouncing of a shield faded, the Scots rushed out of the trees and bushes on both sides, attacking the confused army.

They fought quickly until another horn sounded, at which they stopped fighting and headed for the slope leaving a battered and confused enemy to lick its wounds and work out what had just happened.

Despite being sore from all the stone throwing, she jumped up and down cheering her friends as they returned from the fight; there was Jamie, Belle and Duncan, still alive. She was still safe.

'Aaaa! Let me go!' She was so engrossed watching her friends return from battle that she wasn't aware of the man sneaking up behind her, until he had grabbed her and flung her over his shoulder.

Kicking his stomach and punching him the back, she tried to break out of the man's grip. But the more she struggled the tighter he held her.

'You're coming with me!'

'Put me down!' Mary yelled, kicking him harder.

Then she heard yelling and shouting accompanied by the sound of running feet. Twisting to see what was happening, she tucked her head back in quickly as a dagger flew past her and stuck in the ground a few feet away.

'Leave the lassie alone!'

'Sending a lassie to do a man's job!' her attacker sniggered, as glancing over his shoulder he saw Belle running to Mary's rescue. Bending down he dropped Mary roughly on to the ground before drawing his sword and turning to face Belle.

Free from the man's grasp, she looked around. Belle wasn't the only one running up the slope, all of the men were too but they were heading for the top of the slope, to meet others who were charging down the hill towards them.

An angry cry from Belle drew her attention back to the fight unfolding in front of her. Belle, having reached the stranger, swung her axe at his arm, but the man stepped backwards then quickly leapt forward to stab Belle in the stomach. With a quick twist of her hips Belle avoided the stab and swung her axe backwards so its shaft clattered against the sword blade. The sword shook in the man's hand and for a few seconds looked like it was going to fall.

Mary sat watching too afraid to move, too afraid to speak as axe then sword and sword then axe flashed by.

'Come on, girl, is that the best you can do?' The man taunted as he slapped the sword across her backside.

Furious, Belle turned bringing the back of the axe round across the man's arm. This time she didn't miss and the man staggered back cursing. As she ran at him, her axe ready to swipe at his neck, he raised his leg and kicked her hard in the stomach, sending her reeling on to her back.

Mary wanted to help Belle, but her legs wouldn't obey her thoughts.

‘What are you doing down there?’ he laughed raising his sword above his head in preparation to stabbing Belle. As the sword lowered Belle turned on her side and grabbed the dagger she had thrown earlier which was lying close to her, and as the man bent to push the sword through her she thrust the dagger into his stomach. With an agonising yell he toppled to the ground.

‘Come!’ Scrambling to her feet, Belle yelled pulling Mary to her feet and dragging her up the hill to join the rest of Jamie’s men who, having beaten off the attack from a small part of the English army, who had stumbled across them on their return from searching for supplies, were coming to find Belle and Mary.

Chapter 7

'We'll stop here, catch our breath,' Jamie announced when they had put a fair distance between themselves and the pass. 'Rab, light a fire. Hurry, we can't stay long, we need to keep moving. Belle, you have blood on your face. Are you hurt?' Jamie asked tenderly.

'It isn't mine,' Belle said wiping the blood off her face with her sleeve.

'We can't rest for long. We have work to do. Where's Mary?' He scanned the faces looking at him. Mary was nowhere to be seen. 'Belle, go and look for her. I hope she hasn't wandered off again.'

Belle didn't have to search for long, she found Mary sitting behind a tree. Mary looked up through her tears as Belle sat down putting an arm round her.

They sat in silence until, unable to bear it any more, Mary blurted out, 'Donald's dying because of me.'

'Because of you?'

'If I hadn't been in the woods, you wouldn't have had to take me with you. We wouldn't have stopped in the clearing and.....'

'And the attack wouldn't have happened,' Belle finished for her. 'Hugh and Walter would have attacked somewhere else that is all. It is not your fault.'

'Will Donald die?'

'I don't know. I hope not, not because it would be the end for Duncan but because Donald is a good man and doesn't deserve to die because of betrayal.' Belle turned her face away to hide the tears welling in her eyes.

'Will I see Malcolm again?'

'I'm sure you will. He will be safe in the castle.'

‘If he survived the ambush.' She had told herself that he had survived; that he had been the one watching them ride off. She didn’t know how to express her fear that he was now with the English by choice, so she changed the subject.

‘I can still see the face of the man you killed, I have tried closing my eyes to shut out the image, shaking my head to shake out his face and covering my ears to shut out the sound. I can still see his face and hear his moans and groans.’

A knowing smile crossed Belle’s face as she spoke, ‘I felt just as you do after my first death. The image will fade with time. These are brutal, bad days, death is all around us. With time you grow use to the hardship, the fights, to the injures, to the sounds, to losing your friends and not knowing if you are going to see your family again. You learn to shut it out, to believe that every blow is for Scotland.’ Belle paused for breath. ‘We still have bad work to do, work that you will find painful. Will I see if Jamie or Ian can spare a man to take you to King Robert? We must leave now.’

Mary didn’t move.

‘Mary, what’s the matter?’

‘Hugh told me that my family are dead because of Jamie.’

‘Hugh told you that? Mary, I want you to believe me.’ Belle looked her straight in the eye. ‘Your father helped Jamie and Hugh when they were in danger of being captured by King Edward’s men. He hid and fed them, then helped them return to us. It was Hugh, not Jamie, who told the English knights of your family’s involvement. Hugh killed your family.’

Mary looked at Belle, trying to work out if she was telling the truth or not. Deciding that Belle was telling the truth, she took hold of her hand and went with her to rejoin the men.

'Men, fire!' Jamie shouted, when he saw Belle and Mary return, before along with some of the men he lit a torch from the fire.

'Stay close to me, keep your head down.' Belle whispered as she helped Mary on to her horse.

'Let's ride,' Jamie shouted, spurring his horse and holding a burning torch high above his head.

They rode through the countryside, burning everything in their path. It was not just the fields and crops that they burned but the houses too. Tears welled up in Mary's eyes at the memory of her village being burnt, her home destroyed. These villages were just like hers. At first, nobody stood in their way. Then as villages and towns noticed the smoke and flames in the distance they realised what was happening and set up defences against the Scots. They built barricades hoping that the Scots would go round their village; they were wrong. Jamie's men merely rode down the barricades and the people who had gathered to fight them.

Mary sat on the back of Belle's horse holding on tight, the hood from her cloak pulled down over her face which was buried into Belle's back. She figured it was safer there, away from the axe that was swinging in Belle's hand and the weapons coming towards her from the desperate villagers. It wasn't just their weapons that she had to worry about; some of the villagers tried to pull her from the horse but she kicked out at them and managed to free herself.

When she did summon up the courage to look all she saw was mayhem. Men were fighting; women and children ran in all directions trying to put out the fires, trying to save their homes. Children stood screaming or crying in their mothers' arms. Other women yelled encouragement to their men, one or two picked up discarded weapons and joined in the defence of their homes, others cursed the Scots.

Although the Scots were coughing and choking from the smoke they did not stop. They rode on from village to village continuing the destruction.

Even when they reached Scotland the burning continued. The only difference being that the Scots offered no resistance, they merely gathered together what possessions they could and headed into the hills.

The destruction only stopped when, late into the night, the men and horses became too tired to continue. As their pace slowed Mary whispered to Belle, 'Why did you burn the villages and the crops? Did they hide soldiers too?'

Belle took a few minutes to answer, 'We don't like doing it. Especially not to fellow Scots, they have had their homes and their crops burnt so often. It is just...it is just one of the best ways we have to slow the advance of the English army. If we burn the land, destroy the houses there is nowhere for them to get shelter or food. Therefore when they arrive to fight us they will be hungry, tired and most of the soldiers will want to go home rather than stay and fight.'

'What will happen to the people?' Mary really wanted to ask what had happened to her parents if they had survived the attack on their village, but how would Belle know? Maybe, by hearing what would happen to the people whose homes they had destroyed, she might get hope that her parents were alive.

'They will live in the hills, in temporary shelters. They will return to their homes once the English army has been defeated and be able to live as free people. If we do not defeat the English....' her voice trailed off and Mary was glad that it had as she did not want to hear what would happen to the people if King Robert and his army were not victorious.

The rest of the journey continued in silence until they reached a camp. As they rode into the camp a young, harassed looking man came out to meet them. He greeted Jamie with a hug.

'Good to see you, Jamie and you too, Ian. I take it your trip into England was a success?'

'Yes, Thomas, it was. Managed to take the castle yet?' Jamie asked, jokingly clapping the man on the back.

'No, we have hit them with everything but somehow they manage to stay in the castle. We can talk about that later. But first, you look hungry and tired. Rest, eat, then we can talk.' All but Duncan, who went looking to see if Donald had recovered, followed him into the tent.

'James, you are remiss. I know most of your band of men and women,' Thomas winked at Belle as they settled down to eat. 'However, I don't know this young lass.' He nodded at Mary.

'This is Mary,' Jamie introduced her. 'Her home was destroyed by the English and her family are missing. Her brother may be a captive in the castle.'

'I am Thomas Randolph, nephew to King Robert.' Mary curtsied. 'That is unnecessary. I am merely an earl. Shaking my hand will be greeting enough for me.' She shook Thomas' hand while trying to hide her embarrassment.

'Now let's discuss your problem here, Thomas,' Jamie suggested after they had eaten.

'Are you going to attack the castle? Will you not kill Malcolm?' Mary asked as Jamie and Thomas made to leave.

‘We will make sure that our men know not to harm or kill your brother. Don’t fret, Mary,’ Thomas reassured her; as he and Jamie moved outside to talk.

The rest of the men went in search of friends and family. Left alone, Mary walked around the tent, thinking, she would go to the castle and warn Malcolm of the upcoming attack. There must be a way of getting a message to him. She might even be able to rescue him, bring him back to join Jamie, then they could go together to search for their parents. As she headed outside, a breeze brought the smell of the campfires to her the smell reminded her of the burning villages.

‘I won’t go right now,’ she said to herself and walked round the tent again. When she tried to leave a second time the sights, sounds and smells, the face of the dying man all came flooding back to her. ‘No, I’ll just wait here. I am not even sure that Malcolm is in the castle. There’s no rush. I’ll sit down and think about it, make a plan. Is that not what Jamie would do; make a plan? Anyway, Jamie will see that Malcolm is safe,’ she said to herself as she went to sit down. She had hardly sat down when she fell asleep.

‘Come quickly. Jamie needs to talk to us.’ Belle shook her awake.

Still half asleep she followed Belle outside. Jamie and Thomas were standing in front of the men and women from the camp, who had all gathered together in response to an order. Thomas addressed them.

‘We’re leaving here.’

‘To join the king?’ one of the men shouted.

‘Yes, to join the king,’ Thomas sounded mysterious.

‘What about the castle?’ another man asked.

'The English army are approaching fast. We have to leave here, to get as many men as possible to King Robert. To prepare for the battle.'

'Does anyone have any questions?' When no one spoke, Thomas continued, 'Go everyone, each of you strike the camp. Go now. We leave in three hours.'

They packed up the camp; putting out the fires, picking up the scraps. Mary ran from one group to another helping where she could. Within a couple of hours they were ready to leave.

As they were leaving, Mary thought she saw someone standing on the battlements watching them. 'Is that you, Malcolm?' she wondered. They were marching away leaving Malcolm in the castle, leaving him to the English army. What would happen to him?

They had been marching for what felt like hours, when her thoughts of all the dreadful things that could happen to Malcolm, and why Jamie had broken his promise to her, were disturbed by Thomas. 'We will stop here,' he announced. Some of the men scratched their heads and looked confused. They were only a few miles away from the castle and a couple of days march from King Robert at Stirling.

'If we are marching to join King Robert why are we stopping here?' she asked Donald who, still not fully recovered, walked alongside her at the back of the marching column.

'I dinnae know, lass. It'll be some plan o' Jamie's.'

'Don't set up the camp, we will not be here for long.'

'Won't be here for long?' the men whispered to one another trying to work out what Jamie and Thomas were up to.

They settled down to wait; to wait for what they did not know.

Mary sat on her own her head in her hands. Why had Jamie broken his promise to her? He had promised to help her find her family, yet they had marched off leaving Malcolm in the castle. Why? Had Hugh been correct, was Jamie really the bad one?

'What is wrong, Mary?' She had not noticed Jamie sit down beside her.

She raised her head from her hands. Her eyes full with tears, 'You promised that you would help me find my family. Malcolm is in that castle and you left him there, when you are the reason he is a prisoner!!'

Jamie allowed her to calm down before speaking, 'Your father is brother to one of my servants. Good men both of them. When Hugh and I were caught trying to rescue a Scottish knight from captivity, your father found us a place to hide and brought us food and water. He didn't have to do it. He did it out of loyalty to his brother and King Robert. I saw you that night, do you remember?' Mary nodded. 'Hugh was with me. I didn't know then – although things had started to go wrong – that he and Walter were betraying us. If I had known then I would have killed them myself. It wasn't until after the attack on your village that I learned what they were up to, by then it was too dangerous to kill them out right. All I could do was watch them, bide my time. Try and trap them; in the end they trapped us. Mary, I promised that I would help you find your family and I will. I always keep my promises.' Smiling he walked off and addressed the waiting men.

'Men, any of you with long black or dark brown cloaks bring them to me.'

Twenty or thirty men, still baffled about what was happening, fetched their cloaks and lined up. Thomas selected another ten men to wait behind with them. The others were sent under the command of Ian

McRhuari to march to Bannockburn and join up with the main army.

* * * * * *

Malcolm remembered the day, about a week ago, that the Scots army had arrived. Since then things had been different.

'Finally, they have come.' Simon had said that day as he appeared suddenly at Malcolm's side.

'You've been expecting them?' Malcolm had asked puzzled.

Simon nodded, laughing. 'If Sir Giles could hear you he would know you aren't in league with Jamie. The Scots have taken most of the castles in Scotland. If they get control of this castle, there'll be less places where we English will be safe.' Just as he had finished speaking his sergeant had called him to archery practice.

'That's my fun and easy time over!' Simon winked as he had run to join the rest of the garrison.

It wasn't just that he no longer had the company of Simon, but that the castle had become claustrophobic. Nobody had left the castle since the Scots army had arrived because the Scots attacked anyone who tried. It wasn't only that, the nobles had become quieter, less sure of their victory. More than once he had heard the nobles speculating about possible defeat.

All except Sir Giles, who was quick to counter any defeatism with, 'Our king will be here soon, at the head of a magnificent army and the Scots will be swept away like dust.' The nobles had no choice but to agree as the lord had returned to England leaving Sir Giles in complete control.

Almost as soon as the Scots had erected their tents, fed the horses and settled down the portcullis had opened to allow a horseman, waving a flag a of truce to enter the Scots camp.

The English knight had been met by a Scottish knight, neither of them dismounting; they talked for sometime before parting. The English knight returned to the castle; within moments of his return, the lord with a small party of men rode of towards England. From that moment on Sir Giles, who he had managed to avoid since the ambush, had taken charge. He dreaded encountering Sir Giles again.

His mind had been taking off meeting Sir Giles by the arrival, a couple of days later of a large party of mounted men in the Scots camp. One of the horses held two riders. When the smaller of the two riders dismounted, they were the same size and height as Mary. She was too far away for him to see any details but his heart jumped. 'Mary, is that you?' he said out loud; she wouldn't hear him, wouldn't be able to answer him but he knew that it was her.

Chapter 8

The evening had faded slowly into the night when Jamie and Thomas gathered the men together. Mary was surprised to see Jamie hand some of the men rope ladders and even more surprised when the men took them silently and wrapped them round their bodies for ease of carrying, without questioning.

'What are the rope ladders and cloaks for?' she asked Donald.

'I dinnae know myself. You'll find out when I do,' Donald replied, looking puzzled.

Still unsure as to what they were doing they retraced their steps. When they were within a mile of the castle, they split into two groups; the men with cloaks and rope ladders made their way on all fours to the castle. The rest of them waited in the shadow of the hill, with orders to look for a fire; their signal to invade the castle. If they did not see the fire and the raiding party had not returned by morning, Donald was to lead them to join King Robert.

Donald sent Mary to stand on a nearby rock, from where she would get full view of the castle and yell when she saw the signal.

'Don..!' she started to shout as a light seemed to fly through the air towards her, but stopped when the light died away.

A second light followed, again it quickly faded away. Then another light appeared. This light didn't fly through the air but grew and grew from a small speck, until its bright light flickered and danced on the battlements.

'The fire! The fire!' she shouted, running to alert Donald.

* * * * * *

Malcolm was alone in the tower room he shared with John, staring into the night. The nobles were in the Great Hall celebrating Sir Giles' birthday, celebrating the departure of the Scots, the upcoming battle and their expected victory. John was with them; he smiled at the thought of the nobles who would find themselves the poorer, at John's hands, in the morning. The garrison had been given a day off and apart from the few remaining on guard, all the soldiers were in the guardhouse; the battlements were deserted.

Since the Scots had left, taking what felt like his last hope of escape with them, the battlements had lost their appeal for him. Simon had warned him that things would be different now, the hanging around, the relaxed attitude of the garrison would be at an end. With the battle so close they wanted the fight to begin so that they could return home.

Return home, at least they had a home. They knew where their families were, he didn't. Mary was alive. But he didn't know if he would see her again or where he would go from here.

It was more than likely that he would leave with the English army, maybe then he would get away. But then again, maybe he would be better staying with them; after all they would lead him straight to the Scots.

As he pondered his next move, his attention was drawn to shadows moving closer and closer to the castle. 'The local farmer has left his cattle out, what a fool. He'll be sorry in the morning,' he murmured to himself. Then straining to see clearly, he peered into the distance. There was something strange about the cattle, they weren't moving like cows.

The creatures reached the castle walls and disappeared from view. For what seemed like hours nothing happened. Then a hook appeared on the battlements, scraping along the stone as it failed to find a hold, before being pulled back to earth.

He waited curiosity and expectation growing in him, to see if the hook would reappear. What was happening? Had the Scots returned to take the castle at night? If they had, he still had a chance of escaping. The hook appeared again, this time it found purchase and gripped tightly to the wall. It wasn't going anywhere unless by human hands, he thought.

The hook was followed by men, weapons in their mouths leaving both hands free to climb; once on the battlements the men moved quickly towards the guardhouses. Some of the men, who had bundles of sticks tied to their backs, stayed behind and began building a fire.

Malcolm smiled. The Scots had come back and invaded the castle; he wasn't going to lose this chance to escape.

As he turned to leave, one of the men building the fire fell over the battlements, a knife in his back. The garrison, disturbed from their night off had been roused and were fighting back. The men building the fire, taken by surprise, were easily overcome. As the last man lay dying, a soldier standing over him, he caught Malcolm's eye.

'Fire! Portcullis!' he got out before dying.

'No, don't! It is a signal fire,' the soldier pleaded. 'They must have reinforcements nearby. Don't help them! We're struggling – what with the drink most of us can hardly stand never mind fight.'

He hadn't thought about that, that the soldiers would be having their own party, making the most of their last night of freedom until the battle was over. For some it would be the last party they would ever attend.

That thought disturbed him, the soldiers, his friends were going to fight a battle, were possibly going to die in pain and agony. If he lit the fire to alert the reinforcements some of them wouldn't make it that far. Yet, if these were the same Scots who had laid siege to the castle there was a chance that Mary was with them. He decided that family came first; he would light the fire.

It wouldn't be easy as he would need to go through the castle, across the courtyard, up to the battlements, then from there to the portcullis, passed the fighting and men who may see him as an enemy. He would do it, he would have to.

Anticipation and fear growing he made his way down the tower. He would soon be free; away from Sir Giles. Sir Giles, the image of that man made him think of his bow. His bow. He could use a burning arrow to light the fire. He ran back up the stairs, grabbed his bow, placed an arrow in the fire, waited for it to catch then nocked it in his bow. Then, drawing the bow back as far as he dared he released the arrow. It glided through the air, over the battlements out into the dark night. He prepared another arrow that also disappeared into the night. His third arrow landed in the fire; gradually the embers turned to flames and spread through the sticks. He had done it.

Now for the portcullis. He ran down the stairs, stopping at the bottom and peered cautiously round the corner. The sound of doors falling off their hinges, banging onto the floor, the softer thuds of bodies hitting the ground, the sound of metal on metal and splintering wood came along the corridor. There was no sign of anyone; the fighting had not yet reached the upper levels. He hesitated, unsure whether to go on through the main part of the castle or down the back stairs.

Deciding that the back stairs would be quieter he moved in the shadows. On reaching the top of the stairs he stopped and listened, not a sound could be heard. He would have to move quickly, time would be running out. Normally it took a number of men to open the portcullis, he would have to find away of doing it on his own.

With that thought he reached the bottom of the stairs and ran along the passageway. His mind so focused on the portcullis that he didn't notice the foot sticking out of a door, until he tripped over it and fell flat on the ground; his bow and arrows falling by his side. Before, he could scramble to his feet a hand grabbed him and dragged him roughly through the doorway

He was dragged someway into the room, as he came to a halt a boot kicked him maliciously in the side before crossing the room and slamming the door. The boots turned their back to the door and stood some time not saying a word.

'Get up!!!' Tom hissed as he crossed the floor. 'Get up!'

Bruised, his side hurting where Tom had kicked him, groaning in pain he slowly pulled himself to his feet. Immediately, Tom produced a stool from somewhere and shoved him on to it. His rough hands searched him, found his knife and threw it across the room, where it disappeared into the shadows.

As he watched the knife vanish, he looked round. The room was in darkness; all the lights had been extinguished and shutters pulled over the windows. A gap in the shutters allowed enough light into the room to enable him to see Tom. A low rumble of thunder broke the silence. He shivered, unsure if it was the dampness and cold in the room or Tom's presence that made him do so.

'Trying to escape again?' The cruel smile that made Malcolm want to run him through crossed Tom's face.

'What about you? Why, are you not helping your friends defend the castle? I might have known a coward like you would hide down here.' The sound of Tom's hand, connecting with his cheek resounded round the room.

'Shut up! Not another word!' Tom stomped off and stood by the door.

Shocked, reeling from the slap, his face stinging, his body aching from being dragged and kicked, he sat unmoving, not knowing what to do. If only he had his knife he could try and escape, without it he wouldn't have a chance of overcoming Tom. His only hope now was that someone would find him.

His ears pricked up at the sound of running feet. Tom wrenched the door open, 'The garrison is leaving.' He sounded surprised, shocked even. 'They can't have been beaten, surely?' Malcolm, figuring that Tom was talking to himself kept silent.

Then, with a sudden movement Tom shut the door and pulled him out of the seat. 'Not a sound, you hear?' Tom growled placing his hand over his mouth, dragging him into a dark corner.

He felt cold metal at his neck.

Then footsteps approached the door, paused, the door opened and a voice called, 'Malcolm, Malcolm, where are you?' A figure in the doorway stood looking around the room then disappeared.

'Mary,' he tried to shout but Tom pushed the dagger harder against his throat.

'Not a word!' Tom held the knife to his throat for a few minutes before removing it and his hand from

Malcolm's mouth. Released, he fell to his knees, tears streaming down his face, his neck sore but uncut. With large strides Tom crossed the room and made for the stairs; he returned a few seconds later empty handed.

'Thought you were going to be rescued? Well, your sister missed her chance!' Tom said mockingly. 'On your feet!' Tom grabbed him by the hair and dragged him across the room, down the stairs and out into the courtyard. As soon as they were outside he started wriggling and tried to scream, but his scream was cut short by the point of Tom's knife against his back.

'Not a word, not a sound, you hear? Or I'll use the knife,' Tom whispered, his mouth close to Malcolm's ear. He kept the knife pointing at his back as they made their way to the front of the castle. As they went Malcolm scanned the faces, looking for someone he recognised, Mary, Jamie or even the men from the woods, surely they would do something to help him.

'Neil, over here,' Tom waved to one of his friends who happened to drive by in a cart; he lifted Malcolm into the cart. 'Get us out off here,' he barked as he climbed in beside Malcolm.

The cart jerked forward with a start, bumping and throwing its occupants against the side. Even Malcolm, still being held down by Tom, was flung violently against his captor's foot which lashed out and kicked him. At that moment, lightning cracked across the sky accompanied by an angry roar of thunder and rain that bounced off the ground. Before they had gone through the portcullis he was soaked to the skin.

They joined the remainder of the garrison who, with heads lowered against the rain, were making their way out off the castle. They marched on through the mud, rain and wind until they came across a long abandoned monastery where they settled down for the night. Some of the soldiers tried to light a fire in the hearth; when they finally succeeded the rest of their companions pushed and shoved to get close to the flames.

'Here.' Tom pushed his way through the men hogging the fire and pulled up a chair. 'Sit.

Malcolm sat.

'Food,' a voice shouted from somewhere and Tom disappeared returning later with a bowl of scraps and shoved it onto Malcolm's knee.

'Eat. You need to be strong if you're going to be Sir Giles' squire.' He stood over Malcolm as he ate.

After the food had been served the noblemen, including the commander of the garrison, gathered together talking in low voices that were soon raised as the conversation grew animated. More than once a dagger was drawn. Eventually, when things seemed bad Sir Giles raised his voice so as it could be heard above all else.

'Enough! We are the rule makers, the ones the peasants and lower orders look to for guidance; yet we can't agree on whether to remain here or move into England. I, therefore as the most important knight here, have decided that as the last report we received stated that the English army were marching to Scotland; at a rate which means they will pass this point in a couple of days if not tomorrow, that it would be wise for us to remain here.'

'How will we know when the army is near, they may not pass the monastery directly but may skirt by?' one of the men asked.

Sir Giles gave him a look that said: are you the most stupid fool in the country? The tone of his voice echoed his look. 'Because, we will appoint a lookout and you my friend will take first watch.'

The man looked at the ground. 'As you wish, Sir Giles.'

'Do you think the Scots will attack us here?' Sir Henry asked.

'No, we should be safe enough. They will be occupied with destroying the castle and preparing for their upcoming defeat,' Sir Giles said, knowingly. 'Now I am going to find somewhere to rest. You arrange the watches?' Sir Giles ordered the commander, 'and make sure this man here takes first watch.'

'I will see to that,' the commander said as Sir Giles headed off to find the best room in the monastery.

It wasn't until noon on the second day that one of the men on watch came rushing back into the monastery in search of Sir Giles. He found him in the Abbot's quarters.

'The army is close.'

'Where?' Sir Giles demanded.

'Heading north about half a mile east. They should be level with us in a couple of hours.'

'Inform the men that they should be prepared to leave in fifteen minutes.'

Weary and unrested after their stay in the monastery, some of the men having taken ill, the soldiers that set out were not exactly the pride of England. Yet they marched in order. Sir Giles sent a couple of messengers ahead to inform the English Army of their presence of the men and the rendezvous point.

'Tell, King Edward that Sir Giles awaits him, he will come if you tell him that. He will come for me,' he boasted.

The garrison reached the rendezvous point long before the main army. While they waited, Sir Giles who had spent most of the time in the monastery huddled together with a few other knights making plans, whispering, not showing any interest in the lower orders now took the opportunity to check the quality and quantity of men available.

He came across Tom and Malcolm.

'I told you to get rid of him, not bring him along.' he said to Tom.

'I thought he might be of use.' Tom fawned, not wanting to admit to Sir Giles that he couldn't kill a child.

'Of use, what use could he be?'

'I was thinking you'd need a squire and it would do the lad good to watch King Robert being defeated.'

Sir Giles laughed, 'That would be punishment indeed. What of it, lad? Do you want to help me destroy Jamie Douglas and King Robert?'

Malcolm didn't answer.

'Of course you do!' Sir Giles replied for him before heading off to arrange for the garrison to join in with the main army; that had come into sight.

'Still with us, young Malcolm?'

Malcolm looked over his shoulder to see who was speaking; it was Sir Alexander who he had not seen for days and had all but forgotten about.

'I thought you would have got out of here by now. Ach, well never mind there is still time, you will find a way.' Sir Alexander winked at him then laughed at the look of amazement on Malcolm's face as the English army drew level with them.

The vast column of the English Army with its armoured knights, the different coloured standards and banners of the noblemen, the mass of men and women on foot, dogs running loose and the large, powerful horses, the rows and rows of carts and wagons, seemed to vanish far into the distance.

‘Look at their pomp, their pride, their arrogance. I would bet that those wagons contain tapestries and other furnishing to keep them in comfort while fighting the Scots and to furnish their new Scottish estates.’ There was derision in his voice.

‘Their Scottish estates?’

‘Yes, in their arrogance they have already split Scotland up between them?’

‘They expect to beat us?’ Malcolm queried, fearing that they had no chance against such a large army.

Sir Alexander shook his head. ‘They don’t expect us to fight. They believe that the very sight of their army will be enough to scare us into submission. I hope it isn’t.’

Before Malcolm could respond they were on the move again; the noblemen taking their places at the front of the column the others fell in behind.

Chapter 9

In amongst the foot soldiers the English army did not look so glamorous or impressive. The men were ragged, dirty and tired. They don't look like much of a threat, Malcolm thought. We could beat them easily. If I had my bow I could take out a few of the soldiers around me, now. I would need to deal with Tom first. His hand moved to his waist looking for his knife.

'Son, I wish I could join you in that cart,' one of the solders said longingly. 'My feet are blistered with all this marching. I have hardly slept or eaten this past week. March, march, march! That is all I've done for a week and for what? So my lord and master can get more land in Scotland, so the King can rule the whole land. I have a wife and children. I would rather be with them than here, marching, marching.'

The cart lurched forward suddenly, as Tom whipped the horse and the solider was left behind.

Not long afterwards they pulled into a field to rest. The soldiers fell where they stood. Malcolm sat in the cart, listening for the sound of snoring, the steady breathing of sleeping men and the now familiar snorting of Tom asleep. He sat still until he was sure that apart from the guards, who were leaning against trees or laughing and talking together, all were sleeping. This was his chance to get away from Tom. Away from the hate where he could think more easily, plan how he was going to get to the Scots' camp. He started to climb out of the cart but hesitated when a dog barked. He continued to climb but a horn blew. He hesitated again. Then, as the horn blew again and the men began to stir, he jumped softly to the ground. Clambering to his feet he ran then stopped. Now he was out of the cart, in the midst of thousands of people and not knowing who was friend or foe, his courage failed him. He looked at the soldiers. He didn't know where he was or where to go. He didn't know where to look for the Scots army or for Mary. He would be better staying with Tom until he could be certain of his escape route. He turned to go back to the cart and walked straight into Tom.

'Trying to escape are we? I have a mind to tie you up.' Tom sneered.

'I've been in that cart for hours. I was stretching my legs they were stiff.' Malcolm replied hoping that his face didn't betray his lie.

'I don't believe you.'

'If I was trying to escape why would I have turned back?' Malcolm, proud of his quick thinking, smiled as he climbed back into the cart. Tom stared after him in disbelief, he had been sure that Malcolm had been trying to escape yet here he was returning voluntarily to the cart.

Sir Giles rode amongst the men who were moaning and groaning, shouting at them to encourage them. 'In a few days the Scots will be defeated and you will be back in England, back home. Victorious. You will be able to rest as much as you want. Until then we march.'

Complaining about their too short rest the men formed their ranks and began their march again. Day became night and then day again and still they marched on slower and slower. Until, they came to a sudden standstill. All tiredness forgotten the army had suddenly come to life, talking loudly and excitedly. Following the direction of the soldiers' gaze Malcolm's eyes rested on a group of men standing on the top of a hill. One of the men, wearing a yellow surcoat emblazoned with a red lion, a circlet of gold on his helmet, stood out from the rest.

'It's Robert Bruce!'

‘The King of Scots!’ Men tapped each other on the shoulder and pointed.

‘What’s he doing there?’

‘I don’t know.' This was followed by a gasp.

One of the knights, lance in hand, had broken away from the English army and was charging towards Robert Bruce. The rest of the men, gabbling excitedly, shouldered their way to a better view. All eyes were on the charging knight, willing him to succeed in killing the king of Scots so they could all go home.

Malcolm looked for Tom. He seemed to have vanished. Everybody else was watching the knight. Nobody seemed to be paying any attention to him. He did not hesitate this time. He was not going to miss this opportunity. With one last look around he proceeded to climb out off the cart. He had just jumped to the ground when a hand was laid on his shoulder.

‘Where do you think you‘re going?’ Tom grabbed him. 'Do you think I am stupid enough to leave a prisoner alone?’

Yes, you are stupid. Malcolm thought, but didn’t say the words out loud.

‘Back in the cart. This time I’ll make sure you stay there!’ Tom held Malcolm down with one hand as he produced a rope from a sack that lay on the bottom of the cart and tied Malcolm’s hands behind his back. ‘You’ll no’ be able to go anywhere now.’ Tom mocked. ‘Now, watch.’ Tom placed his hands on Malcolm’s head and turned his face towards the charging knight, ‘watch now, watch the death of our king.’ Tom sounded like he would dance with glee if King Robert was killed.

As the English army shouted encouragement to the knight, Malcolm forced to watch, cheered on King Robert.

‘Cheer all you like, cheer if you must but this is the end of Bruce and Scotland,’ Tom sneered at him.

‘Why do you want King Edward of England to rule Scotland?’

‘I don’t, I don’t want the murdering King Robert to rule Scotland. I don’t care who is king as long as it is not him!’

You don’t sound like you don’t care, Malcolm thought.

He tried to think what to do. He was in sight of the King of Scots and Jamie Douglas yet he was unable to escape. He was never going to get away from Tom. He was never going to find Mary. No longer having anything to lose he wanted to make Tom squirm.

‘Who did he murder?’ He knew. He had heard the stories about how Robert Bruce had killed the man who was his rival for the throne, but wanted to hear Tom say it.

‘He murdered my cousin John, who should have been king.’

‘Do you hate King Robert because he murdered your cousin or because he ruined your chance of being Prince Tom?’ Malcolm felt the latter was true.

Tom’s response was drowned out by cheering from the English army. The knight was halfway to his prey. Robert Bruce did not react – he appeared not to be aware of the advancing knight. Malcolm wanted to shout to his King, to warn him of the danger, but surrounded by the enemy what could he do? He wished desperately for a friendly face. He saw none. The spectators held their breath as the knight, lance now in position came within a few horse lengths of his quarry. Still Robert Bruce didn’t react.

‘Why don’t you do something?’ Malcolm whispered.

He could hardly watch, when at the last moment as if he had just wakened from a trance King Robert spurred his smaller, nimbler horse, pulling it violently to one side as the knight reached him. Unable to pull up and change direction, the knight passed by King Robert's side; as he did so King Robert stood up in his saddle and brought his small hand axe down hard on the knight's head. So hard did the axe hit that the knight fell off his horse and lay unmoving.

'Ye..No! No!' The smile covering Tom's face was replaced with horror when he realised that King Robert was still alive.

'Yes, yes.' Malcolm cheered under his breath.

A wave of shock at the death of one of their own flowed through the English army, their murmurs dying away to nothing. The whole army seemed to stand enthralled, until a couple of knights rode amongst them, ordering the ranks to be reformed and the advance to continue.

Slowly, dejected and shocked, the ranks pulled together and continued their march until a few miles later they were ordered to camp.

Alone in the cart while Tom went to find Sir Giles and get instructions, Malcolm listened to the conversation of soldiers standing nearby surveying the ground on which they were to camp.

'March all this way to camp in mud.'

'What are the nobles thinking? Have they left their brains in England?'

'What do they care? They'll be fine and warm.'

'I thought we came here to fight the Scots, not freeze to death in a bog!'

'Freeze to death? We'll be half drowned by morning!'

'Only half drowned?' They all laughed nervously.

‘I’m not sure whether it is better to drown in my sleep or survive to fight in the morning. Especially after what their King did to De Bohun.’

‘Is that who it was? I couldn’t tell from where I was standing.’

‘It was the young De Bohun, not that he’ll be recognisable with his head split like that.’

‘If all the Scots have that determination we’re doomed.’ They stood silently for a few minutes as if contemplating their doom, before heading off to make camp.

As soon as the soldiers left Tom appeared. Malcolm wondered if he had been standing nearby waiting for the soldiers to leave. ‘Down now!’ Tom commanded. ‘Sir Giles wants you in his tent so you are ready when he needs you.’ He grabbed Malcolm’s hair and pulled him out of the cart. He dragged him through the camp, through the mud and threw him into Sir Giles’ tent.

‘Sit over there.’ He pointed to the corner farthest away from the door. 'And not a sound, you hear.’

Malcolm moved slowly, his legs stiff and sore from sitting in the cart. His head hurting where Tom had grabbed his hair. He felt tears trickle down his face.

‘Don’t try anything. I won’t be far away,’ Tom warned.

The light faded as the night drew on. Still Malcolm sat where he had been told, working away at his bonds but no matter how he tried he couldn’t loosen them. He was trapped, no way out.

His head fell on to his chest and his eyes closed.

'Malcolm….Malcolm!’

His eyes still closed, he listened to the loud whisper trying to work out if someone was really calling his name or if his imagination was tricking him.

‘Malcolm!’

There it was again.

'Wha..!' a hand was put over his mouth.

'Shhh!' John held a finger to his lips, shaking his head as he removed his hand from Malcolm's mouth.

He nodded his understanding.

'Lean forward.' As he spoke, John produced a knife and cut Malcolm's bonds. 'Not a word. Simon is on guard outside.'

'You shouldn't be doing this. You'll get in trouble if Sir Giles catches you.'

'He won't!'

'How can you be so sure?'

'Sir Alexander has invited Sir Giles and the other nobles to a feast,' John said winking.

'What about Tom?'

'Tom's been taken care of. Now not another sound.' The sternness of John's voice surprised him.

Unable to talk, he pondered what John meant by Tom being taken care of. What had John done to him?

'Put these on,' John ordered, handing him a bundle he had left by the door.

Malcolm slipped the quiver full of arrows on to his back, threw the cloak round his shoulders and pulled the hood up over his face, the bow in his hand.

They stood at the door of the tent listening, music, laughter and talking came from a tent nearby. 'They don't sound like men who will be fighting for their lives in the morning' he whispered to John.

'Shhh!' John put his finger to his lips.

They stepped outside. He was free, or at least he was free of the bonds and of Tom. All he had to do now was get to the Scots camp where he believed he would find Mary. To do so he would have to cross the ground that stretched out in front of the camp; ground that would be turned into a battlefield in the morning. The ground was open, with very little natural cover.

Were John and Simon coming with him or would he have to go it alone? He wondered. He stepped into the night; he stopped when a hand grabbed him from behind

'Not that way!' Simon whispered.

'What?'

'We would be spotted for miles going that way and would soon feel an arrow in our backs or be run down by a horse. We're better going through the camp and out the other side.'

Malcolm nodded and let John and Simon lead the way. He would trust them. He had to. But why were they helping him? John, he could understand, he would be doing it because he could, because 'that is the way it is,' as he would say. But Simon? He would be shown no mercy if he was caught. At least on the battlefield he had a chance of survival.

'Keep up!' Simon beckoned him with a harsh whisper.

He rushed to catch up and followed close behind them. Keeping in the shadows, they weaved their way through the middle of the camp. He held his breath, expecting the alarm to be raised at any moment. Not that they passed many people, who would raise the alarm, as most of the soldiers were in their tents, taking the time to rest, catch up on sleep. Those who were still about, sat on the driest ground, around campfires talking or staring into the flames.

With all the bogs to negotiate, the going was awkward, even although the soldiers had covered the worst areas their feet were soaking and the bottom of their cloaks dripping when they reached the far edge of the camp.

'Halt!' the guard appeared from his station, his spear pointing menacingly at them. 'Where do you think you're going?'

‘The king has ordered the archers to form a cordon around the camp, in case the Scots try to attack through the night.’ Simon explained without hesitation.

‘I’m not aware of that order!’ the guard challenged him.

‘The order has only just been given. We are the first of the archers, others will be following.’

‘I don’t know.' The guard seemed to be reluctant to let them out.

John stared the man straight in the eye. ‘Do you want to disobey the King’s order?’ ‘Do you want to be held responsible if the Scots attack in the night?’ The guard moved awkwardly from leg to leg and lowered his gaze. ‘Well do you? I will go back and inform him if you do.’

‘No, no, don’t do that. Obviously the order hasn’t reached me yet. Apologies,' the guard said meekly, stepping aside to let them pass.

‘Hurry but don’t run, we need to get out of here before we are discovered.’ Simon’s whisper was barely audible.

They hurried on in silence until they reached the cover of nearby trees. As they entered the trees Malcolm breathed a sign of relief; they were out of sight of the English Army, the only way danger could come from there was if Tom or Sir Giles discovered his absence. If Tom had been dealt with effectively he would be kept out of the way all night and surely Sir Alexander would make certain that Sir Giles didn’t find out that he was missing. The only other person who could raise the alarm was the guard but would he dare admit to being fooled when he could be punished for it?

He figured that the Scots camp should be straight through the woods. Yet Simon led them on a circuitous route. He would pause, examine the ground, kick leaves and twigs out the way, listen intently, then turn this way or that.

'What are you looking for?' Malcolm asked during one of these pauses.

'If someone has passed this way previously and how long ago. Or what animals have been here and what route they took. So I know the safest route.'

'How can you tell?'

Simon laughed, 'That is why I am here. I was caught poaching on the king's land. I was given the choice of execution or fighting the Scots. I chose the option with the higher chance of survival. If I am going to die I would rather do it in battle or helping a friend. Now quiet, don't distract me. We don't want to get lost.'

Not long afterwards, Simon signalled them to stop and listen. There were voices in the distance, too far away to distinguish accents or words. John and Malcolm stood still trying not to move or breathe, their eyes fixed on Simon who stood, head cocked to one side listening.

'Sir Alexander mentioned talk of a possible night attack. These men may have been sent to check if that was possible. Folly, folly! The men are in no condition to fight tonight. Come, we will go this way. Be quick.' He led them forward then turned abruptly so the voices were beside them; he turned once more so the voices were behind them, fading into the distance.

When they finally reached the edge of the forest two men were waiting for them. After exchanging a few words with Simon, they nodded at John and Malcolm then signalled to them to follow.

'Who are they?' Malcolm whispered to John.

'Servants of Sir Alexander's brother; they have been sent to guide us into the camp.'

'Why do we need guiding into the camp? Can we not walk straight through the camp ourselves?'

'We could but we wouldn't get very far, the guards would spot us and may be attack. This way, this way is safer.'

They followed the men along a path of grass flattened by thousands of feet and hooves, a few minutes later they had entered the Scots camp.

Malcolm took in his surrounding and was surprised at the contrast with the English camp. Here the men, women hanging round their shoulders, were laughing and joking loudly with each other about the feat of their king. Others were cooking flat biscuits of oatmeal or turning meat on a spit. An air of expectation hung over all. A group of young children ran up to them and danced round them before running off laughing. Banners of the noblemen, who were fighting with their king, blew in a slight breeze. Blacksmiths were fixing heads onto spears. Men sharpened their weapons. Again Malcolm thought no one seemed concerned that tomorrow they would be fighting for their lives.

Their guides led them to a tent in the centre of the camp. The man standing on guard nodded and stepped aside to let them enter.

As they entered, Mary who was amongst Robert Bruce's company jumped up, knocking her chair over.

'Malcolm. Malcolm. I looked for you in the castle and couldn't find you.' She ran to hug her brother but hesitated.

'Why were you not in the castle?'

'I was, I lit the signal fire.'

'So it was you! We didn't know who had lit the fire. It looked like all the men had died before lighting it. Well done.' Jamie patted him on the back.

‘I wanted to open the portcullis but Tom Comyn captured me.’

‘That cowardly rogue. I might have known he would have been involved somehow,’ Jamie said.

‘Why did you not join us after the ambush?’ Mary continued.

‘I…..’ he hung his head, ‘I was afraid.’

‘There is no shame in fear.’ Robert Bruce laid his hand comfortingly on Malcolm’s shoulder. ‘I want to hear about the English army. But let’s eat first,' he suggested.

‘Excuse me, Sire.’ Simon stepped forward.

‘What is it, who are you?’

‘I’m an archer and a friend of Sir Alexander’s.’

‘What can I do for you?’

‘Sir Alexander has asked me to pass on a message,’ he said holding out a letter.

King Robert took the letter, ‘Thank you, do you need a reply?’ Simon shook his head. ‘Well, go then.’ Simon and John, nodded their farewells to Malcolm and left.

As, they left Donald entered behind them. ‘Excuse me, Sire.’

‘What is it, Donald? Can you not see we are having a private conversation?

‘I thought you should see this.’

‘You thought I should see…..?’ the rest of the King’s speech was drowned out by cheers from the camp and the sound of bagpipes.

At the noise, King Robert ran from the tent. A large body of men, long haired, hardy looking men were entering the camp. The highlanders had finally arrived. Their leader led them straight to King Robert who grabbed and hugged him.

'Angus, Lord of the Isles! You have come. I have been watching for you these past weeks. Here you are. I knew you would not let me down.'

'I said I wid be an' here I am.' Malcolm was surprised to hear such a musical voice coming from such a rough looking man, 'We were delayed by enemy ships on our way, but we are here now.'

'I'm glad you are here, you give me heart. Get your men rested. They will need all their energy for the battle tomorrow. Join us.'

Accompanied by Angus the party returned to the tent, where King Robert proceeded to read Sir Alexander's letter to his companions. 'If you have received this then Jamie's young friend has arrived safely,' King Robert read aloud. 'The brave young men who brought him too you are John, whose story you have heard from your own connections and Simon, an archer, who like myself is with the English army not through any particular love for them but from necessity. In his case the alternative would be death for poaching. I have done what I can for your cause, therefore; in turn I dare to ask if you meet him on the battlefield tomorrow, I beg that you treat him mercifully. The end is almost upon us; I hope for both our sakes it goes your way. If you are having doubts (excuse my presumption) about fighting tomorrow let me help you make up your mind. I say fight. Fight tomorrow. Fight because they are not expecting you to. They are not prepared to fight as they believe – or believed before this day that they would not need to fight. They are tired and hungry. Above all, they are afraid after they saw you kill one of their own today. I say fight! Your loyal subject, Alexander.'

Malcolm smiled to himself, he had been right. He knew that Sir Alexander had been up to something.

His expression changed to bewilderment at King Robert's next words.

'Fight. What do you say, men? Should we fight?'

How could he? How after all he and Mary had been through. After all the deaths, all the lives and homes destroyed. How could King Robert even contemplate walking away from the battle?

'Sir Alexander has done me good service,' Jamie answered the king. 'His advice has been good and led to many a victory. Go to battle, you may not get another chance like this to fight when the English army is so ill prepared.'

He had hardly finished when Donald entered. 'Excuse me, sire, a few more men have arrived, wanting to join the fight.'

'How many?'

'About twelve, Sire, all strong an' good, one o' them is from my village. Duncan an' I grew up wi' him. He is a guid man in a fight.'

'Twelve more men.' Robert Bruce sounded distant. 'Thank you, you know where to send them. Men keep arriving, yet the English army will outnumber us, no matter how many men arrive. What do you think, men, is it worth fighting this battle? Or should we leave now, retreat to the hills, the forests and continue attacking the English when we can? What do you say, should we do as Sir Alexander says and fight?'

Malcolm and Mary stared at each other in amazement, the king give up, walk away from the battle that would decide Scotland's future? No! He wouldn't, would he? The men standing around looked uncomfortable, uncertain what to say.

'I don't know, Your Grace,' one of his companions said.

'Neither do I,' another one agreed.

'I do.'

'That's Thomas, the King's nephew speaking,' Mary proudly informed her brother. She was desperate to tell him about her adventures, about Hugh and Walter but that would have to wait until they were alone.

Thomas continued, 'We have been fighting for too long. The country is tired and starving. Men keep arriving to fight for freedom. You – we - can not let them down. We must fight tomorrow and if we lose then at least we will have lost fighting. We can hold our heads high, pick ourselves up and start over again. If we walk away now, I fear all will be lost forever.'

'I agree with Thomas.' Jamie nodded at his friend as he spoke.

'I too am for fighting, brother.' Edward, brother to King Robert drew his sword.

'You are always for fighting, Edward. Yet, Thomas, I fear you are right. We have no choice but to fight. I fear losing the battle, losing the war. Do I really have the right to ask the men to suffer, to risk losing their homes, their lives if we lose?'

'You are their king. They will live and die for you and if not, they will die for Scotland,' Thomas encouraged.

'Again Thomas, I fear you are right. Now, rest all of you. We have a battle to fight in the morning. Goodnight.'

Malcolm smiled, relieved there was going to be a battle, they hadn't suffered for nothing.

Chapter 10

There was going to be a battle in the morning. Mary wondered if they would they be part of it. She suspected that Malcolm would be. She didn't want him to be, she had only just got him back and couldn't bear to lose him again. If he did fight, she would pray that he survived.

Scared by the thoughts of what might happen, she squeezed Malcolm's hand as he slept. 'I don't want to lose you again,' she whispered in his ear. He stirred, mumbled something and went back to sleep. Comforted by his touch, she fell asleep holding his hand.

When they wakened the next morning they were alone. A couple of daggers and axes lay beside them.

'Malcolm, Malcolm! Wake up! Wake up!' Everyone has disappeared.' She whispered urgently, shaking him roughly. She sat listening to the silence, wondering why they were alone. Had the English army attacked during the night and taken King Robert and Jamie captive or worse were they lying somewhere injured or dead? Perhaps King Robert had decided not to fight the battle after all and in the rush to distance themselves from the enemy had forgotten about her and Malcolm

'Don't shake me so roughly, Mary, and don't fret.' Malcolm sat up, rubbing his eyes. 'They'll be preparing for the battle,' he yawned, as he answered her unasked question.

'Come on, let's find them.' Relieved she sprang up full of life. Still rubbing his eyes and torn between wanting to sleep now he was safe and not wanting to miss the fight, Malcolm followed her. Hanging a dagger and an axe from their belts they went outside.

'Hello there,' a red haired boy, about ten years old, greeted them. 'I'm William Wallace. The King has given orders that you can watch the armies form up and then you must stay with the camp-followers and reserve soldiers. Follow me.'

William led them to a hill overlooking the battlefield, from where they could watch the final preparations for the battle.

'Look at them!' Malcolm pointed gloomily. The English army with all its magnificence, size and power; made the Scottish army look like a small beggar child, armed with only its fists facing up to a well armed giant. 'We're doomed.'

'Do you think we have a chance against such a large army?' he asked William.

'I don't know. I hope with all my heart that we do,' William replied.

'We will fight with our hearts,' Mary said holding her head high and looking proud. 'We'll win Scotland back or die.'

'You won't be fighting,' William said smiling at her enthusiasm. 'You have to wait here with the camp-followers. Those are the King's orders.'

Although relieved that neither of them were taking part in the battle Mary was also slightly disappointed. After all they had been through they were going to be bystanders to the climax. That night, months ago, when she had been wakened by the armed men, had led to this. If her father and Malcolm hadn't helped Jamie that night things would have been different.

'Look! King Robert is going to address the men.' Malcolm's words turned her attention to Robert Bruce who was moving round to the front of his army where after a slight pause, to allow the cheering army to quieten, he spoke.

'What do you think he's saying?' Malcolm asked William as they were too far away to hear.

'He will be encouraging the men to fight,' William said knowledgeably.

As the king finished his speech the Scottish army advanced. When they had marched halfway over the battlefield, with a deathly silence hanging over everything, they stopped and knelt down to pray.

'Malcolm, the birds, the animals, even the leaves in the trees have stopped to pray for Scotland,' Mary whispered excitedly.

Malcolm laughed and gave his sister a hug. 'I missed you, I'm glad you're alive.'

The sound of thousands of men rising was deafening compared to the silence. Once on their feet, the Scots marched forward steadily.

As the distance between the two armies shortened, the English army stood unmoving until roused by the sound of a horn, they charged.

'What hope? What hope do we have against such a charge?' Malcolm shuddered at the power and speed of the horses. 'The battle will be over before it has begun. What a horrible way to die,' he mumbled sadly.

He couldn't bear to watch as the first row of knights, followed closely by the second and third, clashed with the Scots. Row after row the English cavalry charged yet somehow the Scots resisted.

'How long can they stand their ground against such powerful horses?' he asked William just as the momentum of the charge changed. Hemmed in by those charging behind and hampered by the short distance, knights and horses were forced further onto the Scot's spears. Seemingly unawares of the commotion, knights continued to charge until the battlefield seemed to be a confused mass of movement.

As they watched the mayhem unfolding and as a horn called the retreat they cheered. Their cheer was cut short when they noticed a small group breaking from the main body of the English army.

'No! King Edward has called out the archers,' William said fearfully. 'They are the biggest danger on the battlefield, a hail of arrows can penetrate anything and go through the gaps in the schiltrons. They can kill hundreds in minutes. King Robert must deal with them, or all will be lost.'

As the archers raised their bows ready to let loose the first arrows, the small Scottish cavalry charged towards then. Without stopping, their weapons flashing through the air, they ran the archers down. Some were trampled by the horses, some turned and fled for their lives.

'Get out the way, get out the way,' Malcolm yelled frantically at the archers praying that Simon would survive the onslaught. Mary stared at him, questioningly. Had he gone over to the English after all, was he only with the Scots for her sake?

As the last of the archers fell she cheered, 'Yessss!!'

'Mary! You don't know what you are saying.' Malcolm shot her an angry stare.

'What do you mean?'

'One of those archers was a friend who helped me escape,' he spoke quietly.

'I'm sorry, I had forgotten.' Mary said guiltily. 'I hope your friend is safe. Maybe the battle will be over soon and you will see your friend again.' She tried to comfort him.

'The battle hasn't even started. It will be the turn of the foot soldiers next. They're the ones who will determine the victory,' William told them. Three pairs of eyes turned again to the battle.

They watched the foot soldiers fighting one on one, peasant against peasant, knight against knight. They watched as time and time again the English army tightened it grip on the Scots who time and time again fought their way out. Until the English grip grew tighter and tighter.

'We have to do something! We have to help them!' Mary grabbed Malcolm's arm and pulled him towards the battle.

'Where are you going?' William asked.

'To help!?'

'Help?'

'They are failing. The demons are coming!' Mary shouted, desperate for Malcolm to understand.

'What are you talking about?' Malcolm, having freed himself from his sister's grasp, looked at her as if she was crazy.

'Don't you understand? The English army is breaking through, we are losing. Jamie, King Robert will die and Scotland will be lost forever and the demons will come.' Memories of the attack by Hugh and Walter, of smoke and flames flooded through her mind. They had to do something. 'Why don't you understand?'

'Mary, what is going on? Demons? What demons?'

'We need to do something! We need to stop the English army breaking through!'

'How can we? There are only three of us.' Malcolm looked at William, then back at his sister.

'No there isn't.' She ran into the camp and up to the first person she saw.

'We are losing. They need help.'

'Get awa'!' The man pushed her away.

'No! They need us. The demons are coming.'

‘What are you saying, lass?’

‘We need to help them!’ She pointed towards the battlefield. ‘The enemy will break through if we don’t help them.’

‘We can’t hae that. David, com’n here.’ He called to his companion.

‘Whit?’

‘This lassie thinks we should join the battle.’

‘Join the battle, why?’

‘Cos the English are comin’! Whit aboot it? We could capture King Edward himself.’ He grabbed a staff that lay nearby and swung it at David, stopping it centimetres from him. ‘We could knock King Edward off his horse, like this. Or this. Become heroes.’ The men laughed.

Whack.

‘Impudent oafs!’ an old man who had been sitting nearby sprung to his feet and was raining blows and curses down on the men. ‘I know death and destruction. I know whit happens when the enemy comes. Cowards!’ He stopped hitting them to catch his breath.

‘Whit’s goin’ on?’ The voice of the blacksmith, to whom the two men were apprenticed, was so loud Mary reckoned it must have been heard on the battlefield.

‘This old fool attacked us,’ David said angrily.

‘You deserved it,’ Mary yelled.

The blacksmith, hammer in hand, stood legs astride. ‘Now, lass tell me what happened.’

‘The soldiers are falling, we are losing! We have to do something!’ As she spoke tears slid down her face.

‘And you asked this fool here to help. He cannae even hit a nail.’ The man glared at him. ‘We can’t have the army failing. I will see.’ With that the blacksmith stormed off.

‘Wait, Mary. Wait for the blacksmith to come.’ Malcolm tried to restrain his sister as she headed off into the camp.

‘By then it will be too late. Too late.' She broke away from him, afraid that Jamie and his men would fail and that the English army would break through. She ran onto the next group of people to try and persuade them to help.

Malcolm and William stood looking after Mary then shrugging set off in different directions to help round up the camp-followers.

Mary moved onto the kitchen where the cook was preparing food for the soldiers.

‘They need us. The enemy is breaking through, we have to stop them!’

‘Whit can I do?’ the cook asked.

‘Please help.’

‘Whit you doin’ wi’ that?’ the cook demanded of his son as he grabbed a large wooden spoon off the table.

‘I’m goin’ even if you’re not.’

‘Whit about the food? I need to have the food ready for the king returnin’.’

‘Whit good is food for a deid man?’

‘Your son is right.’ The blacksmith, followed by Malcolm and William, appeared behind Mary. ‘Our country needs us.’

‘I - I suppose the food can wait.’ The cook grabbed the knife he used to cut the meat and joined in with the blacksmith.

Now that the blacksmith had confirmed that the English were gaining ground the other camp-followers, accompanied by the reserve soldiers grabbed, pots, pans and sticks, anything that could be used as a weapon.

‘On them. On them.’ They shouted charging down the hill.

Hearing, then seeing the new arrivals, the English army tired and demoralised fled. Soldiers ran in all directions not knowing where to go. The Scots seemed to be everywhere.

‘They flee! They flee!’ someone shouted. The words were taken up by everyone until the noise was deafening

‘Mary, there’s Sir Giles - the man who enslaved me.’

‘Where?’

‘There running towards us. Let’s get him.’

Sir Giles was directly in front of them, swinging his sword around his head, clearing space for himself. When the swinging sword did not clear a path he pushed what ever stood in his way to the side. He was so engrossed in getting away from the battlefield that he did not notice Malcolm just in front of him until he ducked and rolled through his legs, stabbing him with his dagger.

‘That’s for stopping me looking for my sister,’ he yelled.

Sir Giles grabbed Mary who had not been quick enough to get out of his way and lifted her off her feet.

‘Out of my way little girl!’ he grunted through gritted teeth.

Malcolm stabbed Sir Giles again, harder this time across the back of his legs. With an angry scream Sir Giles dropped Mary who rolled out of the way, picked herself up, drew her dagger and returned to the fight.

She ran straight for Sir Giles, shouting, her axe out in front and thumped him in the stomach with its shaft. ‘That’s for throwing me away like a piece of rubbish!’ She yelled catching him again on the lower back with the edge of her dagger, as she ran by him.

Sir Giles let out a growl as he hopped up and down on the spot, shouting and cursing, his hands lashing out in all directions, trying to grab them.

No matter how he tried he could not hit them. They continued ducking and diving, rolling and twisting to avoid the swinging sword, striking Sir Giles when they could.

'That is for Scotland!'

'That is for capturing my brother and for Scotland!'

His face growing redder and redder, Sir Giles glared down at Malcolm. 'I wish now I had dealt with you earlier.' He made a grab for Malcolm but missed. Mary leapt for his arm but missed – Sir Giles swung him arm back and smashed her in the face knocking her off her feet.

As she fell, dark shadows appeared above her, closing in. Outnumbered, afraid and frightened Malcolm stopped his attack. He froze, expecting at any moment to be run through by the sword of an English soldier. Instead, two Scottish soldiers grabbed Sir Giles from behind and led him away, a prisoner. Ian MacRhuari dismounted and lifted Mary on to his horse. Jamie helped Malcolm onto his horse.

'Where to?' Iain asked.

'The king's tent' Jamie advised.

King Robert jumped aside to avoid being knocked over by Ian MacRhuari, who pushing past him placed Mary in the king's bed. He turned to one of the king's servants, 'Do you know Old Jock?' The servant nodded. 'Well fetch him, man. Be quick.' The servant looked at King Robert, who nodded his approval, then rushed out in search of Old Jock.

'How? What?' The king asked.

'They were fighting Sir Giles. Would have got him too if he hadn't knocked Mary unconscious.'

‘That is what happens when orders are disobeyed! I told them to stay with the camp-followers and watch!’ he said angrily

‘Rumour has it that it was them who brought the camp-followers to our rescue.’ Jamie said, in an attempt to appease the King.

‘I don’t have time for this now. Jamie, King Edward has left the field, running for England. Make sure he gets there. Don’t do anything rash; I can spare only a few men and need you back tomorrow,' he ordered jumping out the way again as Malcolm flew to Mary’s side.

Mary lay in bed, her eyes closed and the colour drained from her face. He threw himself down beside her. ‘Mary, Mary, don’t die on me.’ He pleaded. ‘I have only just got you back.’

‘Will she survive?’ he asked Old Jock who was tending to Mary.

He didn’t get an answer.

Hour after hour he sat beside her bed, ignoring all the suggestions that he should rest.

‘Let him be,’ Old Jock insisted as he placed a cloak round Malcolm’s shoulders.

All through the night, Malcolm sat holding Mary’s hand, listening to her murmur about demons. Occasionally she would scream out.

‘Don’t die, Mary, I’ll protect you from the demons.’ Taking her hand to reassure her, the events of the day caught up with him and he fell asleep with his head on the bed. When he awoke, her eyes were open.

‘Mary! Mary! It’s good to see you.’

‘You too, Malcolm.’ Mary said softly.

‘She is over the worst but needs rest,’ Old Jock informed him. ‘Let her sleep.’

‘I want to stay here.’

‘No, Malcolm. It’s best that you leave her to sleep. Why don’t you go and help the men tend to the injured and the dead.’ Malcolm wondered how such a frail looking man as Old Jock could sound so authoritative.

Reluctantly, he obeyed.

Later, as he was helping to lift a body into one of the carts being used to transport the dead, he caught sight of a man tending to an injured soldier and dropped the body he was helping to lift.

He stared, open mouthed. It couldn’t be?

‘Father?’ he called, cautiously.

The man turned, a surprised look on his face which quickly changed into a smile. ‘Malcolm! Malcolm!’ They ran to each other and hugged.

‘We heard about the children who had rounded up the camp-followers. We thought they sounded like you. We looked for you but couldn’t find you. Where is Mary?’ his father asked glancing around; looking for Mary.

‘I let her take part in the battle. She is injured and dying, it’s all my fault. I should have stopped her, not let her take part in the battle. If I hadn’t pointed out Sir Giles….!’ Malcolm wept as he spoke.

His father shook his head. ‘Don’t blame yourself. I will take you to your mother. Then you can take us both to see Mary.' His father gave him a hug. ‘It’s good to see you. I’m glad you are alive. Your mother and I were worried about you both. We waited at the village for a few days, hoping that you would return; when neither of you did we made our way with the rest of the villagers to join King Robert. We hoped that you were alive. We wanted to believe that you were.' He put his arm around Malcolm’s shoulders as they went in search of his mother, the dead and injured forgotten.

The next day, with the battle over, the prisoners rounded up and the injured having been tended to, Malcolm and Mary who was still weak from her injuries and adventures, stood watching as a long procession of men, both Scots and English, came to make their peace with King Robert.

Sir Giles had already made his peace, now it was Tom Comyn's turn to pledge his loyalty to the man he hated. His voice shaking, Tom slurred and stammered his oath of fealty.

King Robert spoke with anger. 'I accept you to my peace. But you are not only a traitor. You are a robber, a kidnapper, a weak and vile man. You must leave Scotland immediately and never return. Go to your family's estate in France if they will have you.'

Tom bowed, a spiteful look on his face as without a second glance he turned and walked out of Scotland forever.

Malcolm smiled. He was happy to see Tom Comyn being punished and happy to be with his family again.

With Tom Comyn gone and the peacemaking over, King Robert stood up and addressed the watching crowd, 'The battle was won. Not just by the knights and foot soldiers, but by every one of us here. By the cooks, the blacksmiths, the wise women, the children. Especially Malcolm and Mary here who brought the "small folk" to our rescue. We thank you. Scotland thanks you.' The crowd cheered loudly as Jamie and Thomas led them up to the King.

'Scotland and I will always be in your debt. If there is ever anything I can do for you, all you have to do is ask. If you hadn't roused the small folk to action, the English army might have succeeded and Scotland would be on her knees, defeated. Instead she is victorious and can hold her head high. That is thanks to you, Mary, and you, Malcolm. Please accept these gifts from a grateful nation.'

Two figures appeared from behind the king. One carried the most exquisite bow made of the finest yew and a quiver full of arrows. The other held a small hand axe whose shaft had been ornately carved.

'Simon! John!' Malcolm recognised the gift bearers as his old friends. 'You're alive. I was afraid when I saw the archers run over by the cavalry.'

'Meet my two newest recruits,' King Robert laughed. 'Simon is going to help train my archers. After all, we need to do something with all the bows and arrows that have suddenly come into our possession.' The crowd cheered.

Once, the crowd had calmed down King Robert nodded to Simon who came forward and presented the bow and arrows to Malcolm.

'When you are ready, come to me and I will make you an archer in my army. In the meantime, practise. Just don't shoot too many of my deer!' he said laughing. 'John has offered himself as my squire and I have accepted,' he continued. 'Although on the advice of a good friend,' he winked at Malcolm, 'I may find other work that will make use of his unique skills.' He smiled mysteriously as John presented the axe to Mary.

'Malcolm and Mary, the brave young people who saved Scotland!' King Robert presented them to the audience. Mary stood smiling, while Malcolm, embarrassed and not knowing where to look, looked along the rows and rows of faces staring up at him and cheering. There was one face, standing proud, winking at him; Sir Alexander back in the fold.

Later that evening standing in the king's tent, surrounded by the King, Thomas, Jamie and his men, Mary and Malcolm took their leave.

‘Goodbye, Mary,’ Jamie said, hugging her.

‘Goodbye, Jamie.’ Mary held back the tears.

‘Goodbye, King Robert.’ Mary curtsied.

‘Are you sure you do not want to stay and join my army? I could do with two good warriors like you,’ King Robert joked.

‘We want to go home to be with our family,’ Mary and Malcolm said together.

‘We are coming with you.’ Belle, Donald and Duncan appeared at their side, dressed for a journey.

‘You are?’

‘Yes, I have released them to help rebuild your village.’ King Robert said laughing.

Lightning Source UK Ltd.
Milton Keynes UK
UKOW03f2224080714

234818UK00010B/131/P